Love Poured Out for Viet Nam

*First-hand Account of Chester & Mary Travis
and their 50 Years of Ministry
in a Country at War*

TRENA CHELLINO

Living Stones Publications
Pasadena, California

Published by Living Stones Publications
Pasadena, CA
1.800.204.3692

ISBN 978-0-9822124-0-0
ISBN: 978-0-9822124-1-7 (Ebook version)
ISBN: 978-0-9822124-2-4 (Audiobook version)

Dewey Decimal: 266.0231 Christian Missions: Foreign: Asia

Unless otherwise indicated, Scripture quotations are from the *King James Version of the Bible*.

TABLE OF CONTENTS

∾

Introduction

The huge ocean liner coasted slowly into the Los Angeles Harbor. The *USS Grant* was among the last of the American ships to make the voyage from Viet Nam to the USA in the spring of 1975. The city of Saigon in Viet Nam had recently fallen to the North Vietnamese Communists and their Army. Virtually all foreigners were fleeing along with many South Vietnamese who refused to be ruled by the political "hammer and sickle communist" leaders of Hanoi and Moscow.

Among the crew and thousands of tons of freight aboard the *USS Grant* were a husband and wife, both with white-hair, evidence of their years. They were completing their final journey, returning home from the Viet Nam mission field. The irony of this homecoming was that after fifty plus years outside America, "home" had become a different place. They loved Viet Nam so fully as their home that they would choose to die there if the choice were given. But there were children and grandchildren who they loved and needed to engage with before life's closure. So it was that they boarded the last ship available to return to America – reluctantly, tearfully, and finally.

This is the dramatic story of a dynamic couple – Chester and Mary Travis, my Grandparents. What you are about to discover is the story of one of Christendom's great missionary couples. From start to finish they served, side-by-side with their hearts, for over five decades. As far as we know, they never flinched, never doubted or looked away from God's perfect providence and guiding hand.

They committed to missionary service shortly after WWI. Soon after that commitment, they were in French Indo-China (as the country was known at that time) under colonial tension imposed by the French. The early stress that arose would change but never abate.

During their 15th year of service in Viet Nam, the Japanese invaded the country. The Travis family were captured and interned in South Viet Nam. Although their family of seven was never separated or corporally beaten, they were forcefully detained, terrorized by firing squads in the internment camp, and drastically underfed for three years as prisoners of the Japanese army. My father, Urb "celebrated" his sixth, seventh, eighth, and ninth birthdays under the Japanese flag. The American flag he kept hidden in his pants pocket was never discovered.

Chester and Mary served most of their careers in a war zone. After World War II ended, tension increased between the Vietnamese and the French. Not long after the French withdrawal from Viet Nam, the Viet Nam War commenced between the Communists from North Viet Nam and the South Vietnamese supported by the American and Korean troops. Through the years, these missionaries were unflinching, and never looked away from God's providential hand. They never fled from "danger." When explosions occurred and people were running for safety, Chester and Mary ran *into the mêlée* to help the bleeding and dying.

Some labeled them cavalier, even fanatical, as they would praise God while venturing down roads that had been mined with bombs. Year after year they were undaunted by danger and possible landmines which could have exploded at their feet. They drove through heated battlefields and ministered to those in need. They were shot at repeatedly and never hit. Their car tires and windows were blasted as they drove over cluttered roads. Their fellow missionaries and local workers reported that they never swerved or panicked. Their home was shot at more than once.

Chester and Mary Travis became foundational to church history in Viet Nam by risking their lives – similar to the sacrifice Jesus' disciples had done with their lives. Among others, they were pivotal to birthing and developing a burgeoning church that thrives in Viet Nam today under a communist government.

They left America while they were young, handsome, happy and deeply in love. Mary was somewhat angelic in grace and demeanor. She was a loving person. Love motivated her life and it inspired her husband. His grasp of Vietnamese language was excellent, yet hers was a total mastering of the language. That alone attracted the friendship of the Vietnamese people.

He was a high school all-state running back in Indiana during his high school days – fast as a cheetah. He could walk on his hands and even climb stairs as a *senior citizen* doing so. In his later years he would still play football with the younger missionaries stunning them with his agility and strength. He also surprised them with more than ordinary comforting, accepting, and tutorial skills that were especially helpful to younger workers on the mission field. Chester and Mary loved the Vietnamese people without exception – even their enemies, including their captors. They consciously tried to model Christ's example, Who in grace loved all people without reservation.

They departed for French Indo-China in 1924. Fifty years later they were sailing back into Los Angeles Harbor. It would be their final landing after a six-week journey across their personal "Pacific Ocean of tears." They cried all the way "home." They had become somewhat feeble at 79 and 82 years of age, brokenhearted by love for those they left behind in their adopted land, yet bursting with life and joy for their children and grandchildren and loved ones at home in America. The pain of separation from those they loved in Viet Nam would never heal. They prayed faithfully for the Viet Nam people and the Vietnamese church during the few years remaining to them.

From their births in Maine and Indiana, during the close of the 1800's, to their deaths in California, the following chapters tell their story. They read the Bible together, out loud, over 60 times and obeyed it. No reservations were invoked, no hand wringing for security, no calculating for honor. Their lives were demonstrations of "God said it – let's go!" In the history of Christendom, they may not have been outdone in terms of unwavering obedience to the New Testament and length of service regarding the Great Commission. My hope and prayer is that through this biography of Chester and Mary Travis, though no longer with us in body, will give readers resolve to avoid trivialities and take on the courage to do something great for Jesus' sake.

Dr. Drake W. Travis
Grandson of
Chester and Mary Travis

Foreword

Chester and Mary Travis were Christian & Missionary Alliance missionaries to French Indo-China (today known as Viet Nam) between the years 1925-1975. They experienced an abundant measure of Christ's indwelling and overflowing life. One of the aims of this book is to share the unusual experiences and their unshakable faith in their Lord and Saviour.

Chester's pro-football career, with an engineering scholarship at Purdue University, was completely overshadowed by a higher calling, a lifetime call to French Indo-China that lasted over half a century. During that time Chester and Mary raised a devoted family of five. Chester and Mary never missed an opportunity to reveal Jesus Christ as Light for darkened hearts. Their love for the people of Viet Nam and the lost world was the legacy they left their own children and grandchildren and all those who follow them.

Their first assignment was to a forbidden territory in Central Viet Nam as they launched into ministry, seldom lacking an audience. Crowds came to them wherever they stopped during their long trips into the interior. They lived among the people, traveling by car on roads made for oxcarts, and at times crept their vehicle across bamboo bridges. Sometimes they made their own roads or drove across the open fields. They seldom saw their home station. They were called upon to share in the local food cuisine strange for Americans.

They made heaven, as heaven is biblically described, so real, genuine and attainable, that many of the nationals wanted to go there. Many fellow believers did go there, their lives taken by warfare even though they were innocent bystanders. Many believed that the violence would cut short the missionary activity in Viet Nam, but God used all those years of bloodshed for abundant and fruitful ministry for Christ. To thousands of people in Viet Nam, Christ came to overcome the works of evil, and satanic powers as described in Scripture. When a 'hopeless' opium smoker was converted, the experience taught Chester and Mary the ultimate lesson of God's love!

Imprisoned during World War II by the Japanese for three years, they experienced hardship greater than they had known before. Yet when freed they would return to their adopted land and the Vietnamese people they loved. Nothing could dissuade or stop them in their God appointed ministry.

Knowing they would not be allowed to return to the field after retirement, Chester and Mary stretched their last tour of duty to more than twelve years without a furlough. Their passion for the lost people of Viet Nam was overwhelming. One month before the Viet Nam War ended; they packed and said a reluctant and difficult goodbye to the congregations they had led to Christ.

They moistened the gangplank of the *U.S.S. Grant* with tears of love as they parted from the same port through which they had entered fifty years earlier. During those years French Indo-China had become Viet Nam!

Chester and Mary's departure, as well as the departure of other missionary colleagues, from Viet Nam ushered in a new and vital responsibility for national Christians. Brothers and sisters in Christ, whom they left behind, became dependent upon vital and fervent prayer support from the Body of Christ in the Free World. The indigenous church had to move forward without the help of missionaries like the Travises.

If this book does nothing else but generate and stimulate a continuing prayer vigil for those encountering severe trials behind the "Bamboo Curtain," it will have served well. That is all that Chester and Mary might ask of us. I pray that many who read about these missionaries' faith will put their faith in the God who delivers those He chooses, calls, and sends into our world.

This book is written in the first person narrative and largely contains the memoirs of Chester Travis which he wrote after Mary's death. The story is written as Chester told it through writings, conversations, and direct quotes. Other parts are typical of what he would have said, given the situation. Carefully woven into the story are hours of recordings and interviews compiled by his granddaughter, Leslie Travis Hall, and Chester's friend, Howard Pettman. Stories and memories from their sons, Jonathan, Ivan, Paul, and Urban, have also been included. The historical references to Viet Nam and additional research surrounding the war and other events are also added.

There are also numerous passionate poems written by both Chester and Mary. When the author and date of a poem is known, it's noted. When the date and author are not noted, most likely the author is Chester. However, Mary's authorship cannot be ruled out since many times they wrote poetry together.

Chester and Mary read through the King James Version of the Bible out loud together every year of their married life. For this reason, all scriptural quotations are from their favorite version unless otherwise noted.

Trena Chellino

1

Starting Place

They say that some people come into our lives for a reason, some for a season and others for a lifetime; as if by pure chance people come and go from our lives. I can't say that I subscribed to this overall theory but there are certain aspects of it that do seem to ring true. I don't believe in fate or coincidences. I believe in the Lord Jesus Christ as my personal Savior and have since I was twelve years old. I also believe that the Lord is in control of all things in our lives including the people that seemingly come and go.

For some of us, we have had special friends that were in our lives if only for a brief season but their impact on our lives will last a lifetime. This is a story about my encounter with just such a person who deeply touched my life with his during a short season together but my life would forever remain changed. Then years later the Lord would use me to help impact others with my dear friend's incredible life story.

It all started more than twenty-six years ago. In the

fall of 1982 I was a freshman at Simpson Bible College which was then in San Francisco, California. At the time Simpson was a small Christian college affiliated with the Christian & Missionary Alliance denomination, and San Francisco was a sixteen hour drive from my hometown in the State of Washington. How I wound up at Simpson was completely the Lord's doing. There have been at least two times in my life when I knew for certain the Lord was directing me to do something. One was when I attended Simpson College and the other you're holding in your hands and reading.

I went to college with plans for a degree in Psychology and a career in counseling. In my experience, plans that I make, plans that are not completely submitted to the authority of the Lord, rarely work out. I've also found that the Lord usually has other plans, which are far beyond what I could imagine for myself.

That's how I found myself at college, far from home and completely relying on the Lord to provide for all my needs. I quickly found friends which isn't all that hard at a small Bible school and began attending various churches looking for a "church home." One friend invited me to Christian & Missionary Alliance Church in Hayward where his uncle, Paul Travis, was the Senior Pastor. It was a 45 minute commute on BART (the Bay Area Rapid Transit) or better known as the subway, to get to the church and immediately that church felt like home.

It was on that first visit that I was introduced to
Pastor Paul's father, Chester Travis. I don't remember
the introduction itself but if you'd met Chester Travis,
you never forgot him. He was an older gentleman, clearly with many years on him, kind and gentle, and had a
way of attracting people to himself. Everyone seemed to
surround him as he sat in his wheelchair. He could still
get around just fine without a wheelchair but it served
him well as a great place to sit and rest as people crowded around him. There was always a smile on his face and
there was usually a funny story or joke just behind the
smile. He had a way of offering advice as if sharing a
passing comment from his wealth of wisdom.

It wasn't long before I was invited to spend some
of my weekends at the Pastor's home. Rev. Paul Travis
and his wife Ruthie lived in a nice home in Hayward,
California and housed several others from time to time.
Paul and Ruthie's daughter and son-in-law, Dave &
Leslie (Travis) Hall lived in the guest house in the back.
Their niece, Mary Travis and Paul's father, Chester Travis
lived in guest rooms in the main house. Their nephews,
Drake who went to college with me at Simpson, and
Drew who attended Bethany Bible College in Santa Cruz
also spent their weekends in the extended Travis home.
Drew, Drake and Mary are the oldest children of Paul's
younger brother, Urb, whom you'll get to know later in
the story.

Chester Travis was in his 80's and I soon learned that he and his wife, Mary, had been C&MA Missionaries to Viet Nam for more than 50 years. The Viet Nam War took place when I was a young child. History was one of my least favorite subjects but knowing very little about Viet Nam itself didn't keep me from comprehending the sacrifice of their years of service and what it might have cost them.

Mary had passed away several years earlier. Chester lived in his motor home for a while after her death until Paul finally convinced him to move into their home. Chester liked to tell everyone that Paul kept him "incarcerated" in the best room in his house. We would always laugh knowing how well cared for he was in the beautiful Travis home. One thing I quickly picked up on was how this family had spent most of their years apart from one another. It was a welcoming home where warmth and humor were blended in with story after story of life experiences that were shared as they all bonded together. It was also easy to see how their good sense of humor was threaded through the family genes. I spent many weekend hours with this family and Chester Travis quickly became "Grandpa."

I was a fortunate college student in that I owned a typewriter in the days before we had computers. I earned a few extra dollars by typing up term papers for a small fee. That along with a couple of other odd jobs wasn't enough to pay my tuition that first year. After the first semester of schooling my money had run out. In order for me to receive financial aid and grants that I needed to continue at Simpson College, I would need to become a resident of California. That meant I had to live in state for a year and not move back to my home state of Washington to earn more money.

Paul's niece, Mary had recently moved out of the Travis home and I was offered the apartment room over their garage. For me it was the perfect solution to my financial problems and a wonderful provision by the Lord.

Everyone shared the kitchen facilities of the main house and we all became very close during our time together. While living there, Grandpa and I spent a lot of time with each other. His old motor home that was parked in Paul's driveway had become a workshop of sorts. Looking back it was probably a place Grandpa felt close not only to the Lord but it was also a connection to Mary and a place where they had so many happy memories. Most days you could find him in his motor home, writing poems, reading his Bible, praying and sometimes just tinkering with gadgets and gimmicks, or taking a nap. Together we would look through boxes of pictures from his years in Viet Nam; he would tell me stories; or he'd read me the latest poem he had written. There was always something funny he'd been thinking about and he loved to share it. It seemed that Grandpa reflected a lot on the simple way of life he had grown accustomed to in Viet Nam compared to the fast-paced society that the United States had become while he was away.

On days when he was feeling stronger, we would go on bike rides. He had gotten a three-wheeled bike that resembled a tricycle. Grandpa had put an electric motor on the bike, run by a 12 volt battery that would allow him to pedal until he grew tired, then, turn on the motor and keep going. We took long rides all over town. One evening Paul shared how it was a common sight for him to see his dad riding his tricycle down the streets of Hayward. He had once come across him while he was handing out tracts in front of a local bar. Paul had approached his dad to greet him but was quickly brushed off when Grandpa told him, "Go away, I can talk to you anytime. I'm here to talk to the lost." You could take the missionary off the field, but you couldn't stop the missionary from telling others about the Lord as he had done for so many years.

During the years that Grandpa lived with his son, Leslie also began encouraging Grandpa to write down all his stories from their life in Viet Nam. Leslie had two other Grandparents who had also been missionaries and wanted to preserve the legacy, knowing how quickly it could be taken away. Grandpa was aging and it was easy to see that those memories would only be with us for a little longer if he didn't put them on paper.

When he had finally gotten some ideas written down he asked me to type them up for him. Mary had been the couples' typist before she passed away. Grandpa's plan was to write his memoirs for his family and send them to the Christian & Missionary Alliance archive department for safe keeping. I knew very little about the C&MA as a missionary society, or what they might do with his memoirs but it seemed like a good idea to me. I never really gave it much thought at the time.

We went to work in the motor home; me with my typewriter set up at the table and Grandpa lying on the couch with his Bible across his chest. So we started our long journey together as he told me about his life and about Viet Nam and I began to type not having any idea that what I was about to type on paper, would also be stamped on my heart.

2

Early Years

(1897 – 1903)

Morocco, Indiana is a small town of about 1,100 people located about 65 miles south of Chicago. It is a little community situated on the Indiana-Illinois border with a down town not more than a couple of blocks. It was here that I was born on October 25, 1897. My parents named me Chester Earl Travis. I was there, but didn't know anything, so later I had to take their word for it.

I remember a few things from when I was a kid. I had a good dad and mom, Raymond and Viola Travis. I remember my mom being kind of mischievous while my dad was kind of a serious guy. When he sat down at the table to eat, he kept his mashed potatoes all rounded up and sculptured beautifully. Then he'd cut them in little squares ready to eat. After he got it all done, my mom would then reach over and sample the whole thing. I remember that. I thought it was sort of mean of her, but that artistic work he had done with mashed potatoes was too much. My mom was a little mischievous and yet very playful but she was always very kind.

My dad was a conscientious man, strict in his Christian life. He would not do any work on Sunday and many times as a little kid I couldn't understand why he would not even repair broken toys for me on Sunday. He was a carpenter and a mechanic. We lived in a house that he had built. My Grandparents and aunt who lived on the same street as we did lived in homes also built by dad.

I can't remember much more about my dad, for tragedy hit before I was five years old. He was killed in 1903 as a result of a sawmill accident leaving my mom with two little children, my younger sister Fern, and me. Although Fern was a year or so younger than I; she was the smarter one. She passed me up a grade in school. I was so mischievous and fooled around flunking one grade and she went ahead of me. Although it was embarrassing to have my younger sister ahead of me in school, it didn't seem to bother me too much.

My dad's death had a deep effect on me, I never got over it. He watched over me carefully, but too soon that care was cut off, and that had a devastating effect on me. My mom remarried a man named Edward Puett, and they soon had twins, Victor and Vivian. Then about five and seven years later two more brothers came along, Arnold and Ralph, making six of us children in all.

I withdrew into my shell after my dad died and through many years did not readily communicate with anyone. I remember feeling lost, as it were, during those years following his death. I grew up living in unrest and fear so much of the time. It seemed there was no one to help me.

(1904-1913)

During my grade school years I was full of mischief and pranks, always fixing up gadgets and gimmicks to bother and shock people all hours of the day and night. Piles of boxes and other things on shelves in the room next to mine would mysteriously come tumbling down on my sister or anyone else in the room. Any guests sleeping near my room would be awakened in the night by an old alarm clock on the bed headboard, all done by pulling a remote control string, long before remote controls were even thought of. In their sleepiness, they wouldn't know what it was or where the sound came from. I was always claiming innocence for any wrong doing.

I remember climbing around in barns and hay lofts, commonly trying stunts on ropes up in the rafters and consequently taking some terrible falls. I would swing on the rope then try turning a somersault, expecting to land on the hay below, but one time I missed the hay and landed on the hard boards below. My family thought I was half dead. Always experimenting I would get up on the roof of the barn with a homemade parachute. I once put a cat in a basket hooked to the parachute and let him drop. The parachute didn't open, the cat hit the ground with a thud and the kitty didn't want to hang around me anymore.

One day I "pulled a fast one" on the flock of chickens. I dreamed up the idea of putting two grains of corn, one on one end of a string about ten feet long, and the other on the other end, then throwing them down in the midst of that flock of hens. What a circus I had watching them. One hen would swallow a grain of corn on one end and just about that time another hen would latch onto the grain on the other end and run, jerking the grain from the first hen's craw. Then a different hen would grab it and so on, with no end of swallowing grains of corn and still losing it. That was akin to human endeavors, just as crazy as chickens! They think they've got it made, but in a selfish world, someone else jerks it away from them and runs, only to meet the same fate.

My folks always had a lot of chickens around and they would get huge baskets of stale, moldy bread from bakeries, and store it in the hayloft to feed the chickens. One day, we were up there tossing those loaves of bread seeing how many we could keep in the air at once. There was a big door behind me, and as it happened, I caught a loaf of bread and tried to grab another near the door, but went out the door backwards. They found me 18 feet below, knocked unconscious. They said it looked like I was through, but I came back to life, pretty badly beaten up for the summer. The Lord had a plan and was so patient and gracious with me. He had a purpose that I never realized until many years later. How good it was that God stepped in and delivered me from such futility. To tell any more of these stories would not enhance my background, so you can imagine the rest.

3

The Call and a Companion

During my high school days (1914-1918) I suppose everybody thought I was a good boy, but that was not always so. I was still up to mischief and fooled around with the gang, playing football. I had to keep my grades up in order to play on the team. I succeeded and played fullback starting in eighth grade and continuing through high school. Our team was always getting hurt. We didn't wear pads or helmets in those days. I still have a few souvenirs from back then, one over my left eye and one on my right ankle. I could have gotten my ankle fixed, but the doctors in our "one-horse" town were disgusted with guys playing football. They thought that it was an "appalling game." So the ankle went without medical attention.

It was a small high school, only about ninety students in all, but we were a tough bunch. We hardly ever lost a game. We would humiliate the big Emerson school of Gary, Indiana, every year. Still, with their publicity, they claimed state championship and that would burn us up, so we would go back and beat them again the next year.

All through high school, friends would ask me what I was planning to do with my life. Of course, I was certain I was going to college to play football. I was playing in a game when scouts from Purdue came to watch. One scout said, "Come on down, join the team. We'll take care of you. It won't cost you anything." I really expected to go to Purdue in West Lafayette, Indiana.

I also had a lot of interest in engineering. From my earliest years I was mechanically curious always figuring out how things worked. Hence, I held a lot of promise at engineering as well as football. At age 17, on August 31, 1915, I registered with the US Patent office an explosive-engine that I had invented. I was always fixing, inventing and building new things. Little did I know at the time that the Lord had other plans with those inventive skills and engineering mind!

About the second year of high school some interesting things began to happen. I had professed to be a Christian at about age 14, but had not grown much in my faith until a Baptist preacher came to town to pastor our church. He really began to turn things, not upside down, but right side up, in Morocco.

I began to face some realities. He was preaching everywhere: in restaurants, street corners, special open air meetings. "For what is a man profited, if he shall gain the whole world, and lose his own soul?" (Matthew 16:26) I started to figure that the life I was planning with all its glamour was not worth it. Still, I thought I could go to Purdue for a few years, play football, major in electrical engineering and then become a preacher.

In the meantime, this Baptist preacher persuaded me to go for the summer of 1918 to Moody Bible Institute. He was from the Moody Bible Institute and he was anxious to get me there, knowing it would have lasting effects, and it did. I thought I would go down for the summer and then I would leave in the fall to go play football at Purdue.

Moody Bible Institute (MBI) was founded by evangelist and businessman Dwight Lyman Moody in 1886. D.L. Moody established MBI for the "the education and training of Christian workers, including teachers, ministers, missionaries and musicians to completely and effectively proclaim the gospel of Jesus Christ."

Moody grew up in Northfield, Mass. and moved to Boston in his late teen years. While working in his uncle's shoe store, Moody became a committed follower of Christ and accepted Jesus as his personal Lord and Savior.

Shortly thereafter, Moody moved to Chicago, intending to continue his successful business career. While in Chicago, his passion for education grew, and he began a Sunday school for children. Eventually this school turned into a much larger endeavor, and he left the business world to dedicate his life to ministry.

With the encouragement of others, Moody began to expand his efforts. In 1886, at a gathering promoting city evangelization, Moody said, "I'll tell you what I want, and what I have on my heart. I believe we have got to have gap-men to stand between the laity and the ministers; men who are trained to do city mission work. Take men that have the gifts and train them for the work of reaching the people." This vision would soon birth the Chicago Evangelization Society, later renamed the Moody Bible Institute.[1]

So I went to Moody Bible Institute and never got away. Jesus got hold of me there and would not let me go. How good of the Lord to just fence me in. It reminds me of the song "Don't fence me in." I was glad that the Lord did the fencing, on both sides, creating a corridor. Psalms 139:5-6 says, "You have hedged me behind and before, and laid Your hand upon me." (NKJV) That was the way I went! I didn't turn back! So life has been so glorious just because I did not turn back but continued on as the Lord, fenced me in step by step.

My parents did not stand in the way to prevent me from going to Moody Bible Institute, although they didn't understand why I wanted to give up a career in electrical engineering that I would have had by going to Purdue. Once I got the power of the Holy Spirit down deep in my heart, there was nothing else I could do. I had no doubt the Lord charted my course.

Then something wonderful happened to me at Moody. Sunday was the busy day for going into the city for evangelism, so Monday was the day to relax by going to parties and on picnics.

While at Moody I was a loner. I didn't go out on many dates. I was there for no more than a year when I met one of the most precious women in all the world. That is what it took to get a tin-horn sport like me to shape up. And for this woman I had to shape up because she was a very attractive New Englander.

I feel the Lord kept me from going with many girls. I'm thankful that by my second year in high school most of the girls thought I got too much "religion" to suit them, so they didn't fall for me. I was very outspoken and too sure of my religious convictions. At times I felt completely left out.

After about a year at Moody Bible Institute I was surprised when one group asked me if I would like to go on a trip with them to a place called Mayfair, way out in North Chicago for a picnic on our Monday off. What a day that was for me! While lumbering along in that old clanging street car I saw a beautiful maid sitting alone in one of the seats. Boy, what an invitation! I mustered up enough courage to go over and sit down beside her. As I said, she was so attractive.

We had a good time that day with the crowd and I never thought much of it, and never thought I had made any kind of an impression on her. We hung around together a lot that day and it lasted until evening when I finally walked her to the women's dorm at Moody Bible Institute. No doubt, I thought, that was the end of it. I figured it was just a friendly day together and then "curtains." Then as I was about to leave, I saw a little piece of driftwood that she was clutching in her dainty little hand. I said. "What's that?" as she bashfully tried to hide it. I persuaded her to give me an answer and she finally admitted it was a souvenir of that very special day. Well, what do you know? Something had really happened that day and it was so good. The Lord was working with a far more reaching effect than we could ever realize. That day a relationship began that never ended. What strange ways the Lord works. You can perhaps guess the rest of the story; it's like a fairy tale, but true. Right there I took courage to ask for another date the following Monday.

(1919)

Every day in the midst of the throng of students, Mary and I would meet. In classes I would find where she sat, so I could see that beautiful face and deep dark brown hair. We had our regular Monday outings together, always conscious of the Lord's presence, and all our fellowship together was made so meaningful by putting the Lord first in everything. Most of our Mondays were spent in one of the beautiful parks such as Lincoln Park in North Chicago. There we would sit around enjoying each others company, hold hands and look - not always at the park scenery either! We'd go together up to the Moody Church in Chicago where Paul Rader was the pastor. He later became the President of The Christian & Missionary Alliance which seemed so strange because we knew him, but I'll come to that later on in the story. We'd walk up there and back again on Sunday evening, and on Mondays for another picnic.

One evening, I got up courage and asked her to be my wife. I thought surely she would just fall into my arms and say "Yes." Me, a young buck, with such wonderful characteristics like I had, surely she couldn't say "No!" But she did! That was the oddest thing to me, to think that she did not want me, how could it be? I was so disappointed and bewildered. I couldn't understand. What could be the reason? But I was not going to give up.

The next Monday in about the same place in Lincoln Park while we were eating an egg-and-tomato sandwich, I got on my knees and asked again. She had just one question that had to be answered: "Are you going to be a foreign missionary?" The only thing that was keeping her from saying "yes" was that she didn't know if I was going to be a missionary or not, and she was determined she was going to be a missionary!

Then it all made sense and something good began to happen. I said, "I sure am...you remember just the other day when Dr. Samuel Zwemer came from the Moslem world and he made an appeal for volunteers who would go to the mission field? That night I raised my hand and volunteered." There were more than a hundred other students that were there. They didn't all raise their hands, of course, but I didn't know at that time that she had done the same thing. We fell into each other's arms as she burst forth with the exclamation, "That was the very night I volunteered, too!" That was it. If I was not going to the regions beyond, she would have to go without me. Mary was so sure of herself. Oh what dedication! And so it was from then on.

Mary Nellie Hall was four years older than me, born on December 11, 1893, in Fryeburg, Maine. She graduated from Moody two or three months before me, always ahead of me, of course. She, in the meantime, had gone back to Maine during a three-week vacation. I thought she'd never come back. When she came back we decided to get married. I wrote the following poem to Mary in 1919:

> *As twilight softly gathers,*
> *The shadows steal around;*
> *Where a lonely one is sitting,*
> *On a railroad bridge he's found.*

All nature bows her head in rest,
The birds and beast and flowers;
But he alone with just his thoughts,
Must while away the hours.

They turn not to the village near,
A mile or so away;
But rather to the distant east,
Whence comes the dawn of day.

And there from out a weary flight,
They soar to plains below;
And nestle in the hills of Maine,
Where Saco waters flow.

He sees a maiden strolling there,
Head bowed in lonely dreams;
Perhaps of one far to the west,
If so, how good it seems!

In fancied art their paths are near,
And cross upon the hill;
They meet again neath moonlit skies,
While hearts with raptures thrill.

She stands amazed at love's surprise,
Then yields to his embrace;
And timidly she lifts her eyes,
And looks into his face.

The rest cannot tell, just now
"Continued" says the moon;
For interruption comes his way,
Why should it be so soon?

He stands with broken dream, that's all,
And heaves a lonely sigh;
To think he had to break the scene,
To let a mail train by.

It speeds across the country bridge,
And glides o'er hill and plain;
Perhaps it brings a note of love,
From one in Fryeburg, Maine.

At this his face lights up in joy,
And glows in ruddy cheer;
Praise God, it is a note of love,
From his own Mary dear.

We wanted to get married and be ready to go just as soon as we got out of Moody Bible Institute, but there was a rule that didn't permit students to marry while in school. So I wrote a letter to the faculty informing them that most missionary societies require that their candidates be married at least one year before they go to the mission field, and we had volunteered to go to the mission field. We'd like to get married during our last term so we would have that year over and be ready to go the mission field. While this was a stretch it was true. To our overwhelming surprise, the answer was a glorious, "yes!" I don't think anything ever happened like that before or afterwards.

It was just wonderful that Moody Bible Institute would allow us to get married while at the school. One of the teachers agreed to marry us, and what a wedding it was on April 20, 1920, when I married Mary Nellie Hall. Oh, the guests who were there you could count on two fingers; my mother and Mary's best girlfriend, Annie Ludwig. The wedding look place across the street from the school in Mr. Stevens' home. Although we didn't have a big ceremony you don't need a crowd to tie a good knot. The honeymoon was a walk across the street to an apartment that the management of the school had prepared for us. What kindness and thoughtfulness on the part of everyone in that school. Only the Lord could so coordinate everything so perfectly.

Grady Mangham, missionary colleague, later recounted this event in Mary's life when he wrote: "Mary Hall was born on a farm in Maine, and she was ever a New Englander. The influence of her Christian home molded her life during her youth. Trained as a teacher, a profession which she followed for three years, she left a good position to enter Moody Bible Institute in response to God's call. Two wonderful things happened there, which were to affect her entire life. She heard the pleas of returned missionaries—felt the call—counted the cost—and said, 'Here am I, Lord, send me to the uttermost parts of the earth if it is Your will.' The second event took place on her graduation day when she was married to Chester Earl Travis."

4

Preparation for the Ministry

I worked for Marshall Fields as a maintenance man and did odd jobs at the institute while I finished up my schooling and Mary ran the elevator. We were able to get along fine. We married with no reception, and no honeymoon except the moon only, and we had no money! Oh, but we were rich. We had one of those hump-back trunks and all we had in it was a little junk. We had no money, and no place to go, yet we were committed to going to the mission field; but had no idea how we were going to get there. We had enough money for our train fare to Morocco, Indiana, my birthplace, and to my Grandma, who was living alone in the house that my father had built to live in, but never did.

We wanted to go to Fryeburg, Maine, to see Mary's parents, but it's a long way from Indiana to Maine. Since we had no money, I got a job on the railroad, tamping ties and driving spikes during the summer of 1920, and finally amassed enough fortune to get two tickets to Maine in the fall of that year. My wife was anxious to show off the specimen she had picked out in Chicago and reveal that "crazy guy" from Indiana to her family in Maine.

Mary's parents, John and Netti Hall, were really old-time New Englanders. Mary was the second of six children, so there were also five other siblings to meet. Evie was the oldest, next was Mary, then came her brother Alonzo, who they called Lon. Then her sister Angela or "Gela" as they called her, next was her brother Urban, and then John who was the youngest. It was good when we arrived it was still night, as I didn't look too promising. I had to learn their language. Maine, like down south, is different, especially in the way they speak. But, I loved it anyway! What a delight to hear my wife speak with a New England accent all through the years.

Mary's father, Jonathan Woodman Hall, was a farmer. Both of her parents were Christians and she had the benefit of a Christian home and the influence of godly parents. As a family, they had always gone to church, Sunday school, and evening prayer-meeting. Mary's earliest recollections of home were morning prayers with the whole family gathered around the big family Bible. At around the age of 13 when an evangelical preacher came to their Methodist Episcopal Church and preached from God's Word that "all have sinned and come short of the glory of God," Mary was convicted and saw the need of a Saviour. She can plainly remember how she went to the altar with warm tears of repentance that flowed down her cheeks when she accepted Jesus Christ as her personal Saviour and went home as a "new creature" in Christ Jesus. *Therefore if any man be in Christ, he is a new creature: old things are passed away; behold, all things are become new. 2* Corinthians 5:17

Fryeburg, Maine, is out in the country. The next morning when I got up and looked out the window, I saw mountains for the first time in my life. Being from the prairie and corn fields of Indiana, I had never seen a mountain! They were beautiful snow-capped mountains. I gazed on those mountains and on Mount Washington with total amazement!

While in Fryeburg during the coming winter, I preached in different churches and scrounged for jobs in the community. We lived with Mary's parents for a year. In the meantime our little girl, Evangel Mary, came along on February 9th of 1921 to brighten our home and she was so glad and content to go with us wherever we went.

Mary's folks belonged to the Methodist Episcopal Church and the District Superintendent suggested I take a church in that area. So I took a pastorate in Kittery, Maine, where God blessed us and made us "more than conquerors" over a multitude of troubles in that church.

As pastor, I soon found out that the officials of this church were not in agreement with the Bible on issues of water baptism and the second coming of Christ. I believe the Bible as the Word of God, and that it is inerrant in its entirety.

(Spring 1922)

It seemed that the work of the enemy was to keep us from going to the mission field. We were mindful of our commitment to the regions beyond as missionaries, but we were not getting there. The Lord provided a Baptist preacher who often visited us and we had many good "heart-to-heart" talks. One day while talking, I told him we had volunteered for foreign missionary work, but were getting nowhere fast. If we did not find a way to get out, the opportunity would soon be gone. I told him, "Time is running out. If we get too much older, we won't be accepted and we won't get to the mission field at all. We certainly want to do what we promised the Lord we'd do but we don't have any idea how to get to the mission field." I was already 25 years old, Mary was 29, and that was already considered "late" in going to the mission field. He thought a few moments and then said he knew of a wonderful mission called The Christian and Missionary Alliance and that I should get in touch with them. He told us Paul Rader had just become President of the Alliance and was in Boston for special meetings and I should go and get in touch with that society.

We knew Paul Rader from our days at Moody Bible Institute, so I went to the Alliance Rally in Boston and was deeply impressed. I felt like that was one of the most wonderful meetings. I had never seen anything like it in all my life. It was filled with an enthusiastic crowd emphasizing missions and looking for recruits who would go to the mission field. Boy that was certainly thrilling to hear! We had longed to work for an organization in which we could feel free to proclaim the whole council of God and at the same time have perfect fellowship upon which God could smile. The C&MA was founded by A.B. Simpson and has a four part distinctive: Jesus Christ our Saviour, Sanctifier, Healer, and Coming King. That surely was a day the Lord had made!

As it was, I had sugar diabetes and I didn't look like much of a candidate for the mission field. I was on a very strict "no sugar" diet and taking medicine to control it. At the conference they had healing meetings, something I had never seen before. They used to do that regularly. "Around the beginning of the 20th century, A.B. Simpson conducted a weekly healing service that was the largest midweek religious gathering in New York City. At Berachah Hall, the Alliance healing home, the deeper life conferences and missionary conferences spread the message of Christ our Healer across America in the first decade of the movement."[1]

This was one of those healing services led by Paul

Rader. I went down, not knowing much about it, but I went forward, kneeled and was anointed and prayed for. They had told me I could give up the medicine I was taking. I took the Lord at His Word and went home, forgetting all about that medicine which I had been taking. My sweet wife was wondering what happened, so I told her, "I was anointed and prayed for and I believe I was healed." And I was healed!

While we were at Kittery, I got my first car. I bought a Model T, an old second hand rattletrap for $135. That was the beginning of my love of cars. It wasn't long before I was under the thing, fixing it and working on it.

After the Alliance Rally in Boston I felt I could not remain in a church that did not strictly adhere to Scripture, so I notified the denomination that I would be leaving. We were qualified to preach in any church or denomination because Moody Bible Institute was an interdenominational school that taught the Bible. The District Superintendent, under whom we worked, tried many times to persuade us to stay with them, but I had to frankly tell him we could no longer conscientiously identify ourselves with ministers who were antagonistic to the fundamentals of the precious Bible they should be preaching. We resigned from that denomination and went out with open hearts to be guided by God. We believed the steps we took then were ordered by the Lord. We were "anxious for nothing, but in all things by prayer and supplication, with thanksgiving were letting our requests be made known to God, and the peace of God that passeth all understanding was keeping our hearts and minds through Christ Jesus our Lord." (Philippians 4:7)

Many years later the Kittery First Church would note in their Historical records about our days there:

In April 1921, Chester E. Travis came to take up the work of Kittery First Church by appointment of the Maine Conference. He came with determination "To preach Christ, and Him crucified" to his people and this has been the underlying theme of all his sermons.

He, with his wife and baby, were most cordially welcomed and found themselves very comfortably situated in the parsonage, a portion of which had been redecorated and furnished by the Ladies Aid.

The church was found in very good financial condition, but sad to say the spirit of the old trouble was still lingering in the hearts of some which manifested itself in a very unpleasant way when the pastor put on an intense Evangelistic program Sunday evenings; a minority of church members failed to cooperate, but the interest of the community as a whole was remarkable. The Gospel has shown its "drawing power" by the increase in attendance from ten or twelve on Sunday evenings to forty or fifty.

Two persons have accepted the Lord Jesus Christ as their personal Saviour and it is the prayer of the pastor that the next shepherd of this flock may reap much more fruit from the seed that has been sown this year, the Word of God.

The work among the Girls has been a source of great pleasure and blessing to the pastor's wife. The Girls have heartily cooperated with her efforts and in the future show promise of being real workers for the Master.

It is with mingled feelings of sadness and joy that the pastor and his wife leave this charge, sad to leave the people whom they have learned to love, and rejoicing in the hope of soon being out in the "regions beyond" preaching the "unsearchable riches" of Christ to the ones in heathen darkness.

So, we got in the old Model T, left Kittery and went back to Fryeburg, Maine, hardly knowing what to do next. My wife's parents were always welcoming and happy to have us. We decided to start out across country to Indiana to find out what the Lord had in mind for us. In the meantime, I wrote a letter to the President of the C&MA, Paul Rader, and told him we wanted to go to the mission field but didn't know how to get there. His reply was, "Come to Nyack, New York, and the Missionary Training Institute." That school was the forerunner of the present Nyack College and Alliance Theological Seminary.

That summer I got acquainted with the United Brethren Church and they gave me a good job for five months at Wallow Lake, Michigan, a summer resort. The thought of a country boy like me going up there for a summer resort church was unbelievable! I worked for five months and picked up $500. That was a pile of money in those days and we saved enough to get to Nyack.

We had our second-hand Model T Ford and with the money we had earned that summer and Evangel, now about 18 months old, we started across country from the Midwest to Nyack, New York. We arrived there after a tough trip—no freeways in those days, just finding our way driving through the wilderness. We didn't have maps, just heading east driving through every town. We finally breezed in there feeling like the most unlikely candidates for the mission field. They looked at us and probably thought we were a couple of waifs, but they took us in so kindly and cared for us.

The Missionary Training Institute located in Nyack, NY, a suburban community overlooking the historic and picturesque Hudson River Valley, just 25 miles north of New York City, was the first Alliance school, established by Dr. A.B. Simpson. The Missionary Training Institute had its historical roots in the work of its founder, Dr. Albert B. Simpson, who pastored in New York City and founded two organizations, one a deeper-life fellowship "The Christian Alliance" and the other a missionary-sending agency, "The Evangelical Missionary Alliance." Dr. Simpson sensed a need for the two to become one, and in 1887, they became "The Christian and Missionary Alliance."

Dr. Simpson organized the institute in New York City in 1882 to train missionaries. The school moved to the village of Nyack, New York, in 1897 and in time became Nyack College. Dr. A.B. Simpson had passed away just a few years earlier in 1919 but to the end he remained devoted to Christ, and by extension to all who dared to take the gospel message to a lost and dying world.[2] He was a man of vision and faith, and that was the very vision and faith we were looking for.

Mary and I were hungry for an association who believed the Bible and had a missionary program with a vision. At Nyack they taught the Bible. It was there that we really got strengthened in our faith. Those years were a momentous time when we fully yielded our lives to the Lord and clarified our missionary vision. The words of A.B. Simpson in his hymn, "The Regions Beyond" were clearly how we felt:

> To the regions beyond I must go, I must go,
> Where the story has never been told;
> To the millions that never have heard of His love,
> I must tell the sweet story of old.
> To the regions beyond, I must go, I must go,

Till the world, all the world,
His salvation shall know.

"The Regions Beyond"
by A.B. Simpson 1843-1919
Hymns of the Christian Life, p. 460.

At Nyack we were trained and would be examined to see if we were prepared to be Alliance missionaries. Before long they asked us to come before the Board of The Christian and Missionary Alliance for examination. They had us write a doctrinal statement to see how we lined up with the Alliance. They must have been in desperate need of missionaries to latch onto the likes of us. I wrote the following in my application statement regarding the Full Gospel: *I believe the Full Gospel as preached by the Alliance is Scriptural and the most Christ honoring message proclaimed in the world today.*

I believe that through faith in His blood, His death on Calvary, we have remission of sin. On this ground, and only this, God can be just and the Justifier of the believer. On this ground the guilt of all sin and its penalty is put away. Christ is the Sanctifier, setting the believer apart as His child, beginning a good work in him that He will continue until the day of Christ. This good work is setting the believer apart more and more from sin unto a holy life. Not that quitting a certain sin is a gradual process, but that God keeps revealing all our seeming most insignificant sins that we might confess them and go from glory unto glory, growing in grace and the knowledge of our Lord Jesus Christ.

Concerning Christ our Healer, I believe in the promises of God, provision is made for the healing of the afflicted in Christ, Christ Himself being the Healer. I take Psalm 103:3, James 5:14-16 and 1 Corinthians 11:30-32 at their full value. He can do this since it was paid for in the Atonement.

I believe Christ is coming at the end of this Church Age to take out His own people, those alive and those whose bodies are in the grave. We shall all be caught up to meet Him in the air and shall ever be with Him. The Holy Spirit shall also be taken, then Satan and the Antichrist shall be unrestrained in the awful tribulation. After this Christ shall come for a thousand years' reign of peace and righteousness. This is the one and only hope of peace in this sin-cursed, war-torn world, and while earnestly laboring to save men, we pray "even so, come, Lord Jesus."

While we were at Nyack awaiting our appointment, the Superintendent of the South American field was there and we met with him and found it quite interesting. It was suggested we prepare to go to South America. That sounded good, not too far away, back home in a few hours, not bad at all. We didn't want to go too far away anyway. But that was not the Lord's plan.

We signed up and took one lesson in Spanish. I didn't become fluent in that one lesson. Language was not my "line." I spent four years getting through two years of Latin and just barely got it. I didn't care a thing about language. I knew a lot more about physics, engineering and things like that, but no "language" for me.

In the meantime, Dr. A.C. Snead, the Foreign Secretary of the Alliance, and the representative for the Far East including French Indo-China, approached me. He handed me a small pamphlet, "The Call of French Indo-China," and asked us to consider going there. We looked it over and recoiled from the idea because we thought that place, French Indo-China, was "out of this world." We had no idea where it was. Where was that place all the way on the other side of the earth? No one had ever heard of it.

Indo-China is a term applied to the great peninsula of the southeast corner of Asia, south of China and east of India. It has sometimes been called Farther India, but it is not a part of either India or China, and is subject to neither of those countries.

The peninsula of French Indo-China was a vast area made up of a group of French protectorates and colonies which some years later was recognized as six mission fields in one. It comprised five great states, Tonkin, Annam, Cochin-China, Cambodia, and Laos. The first three, Tonkin, Annam and Cochin-China are Viet Nam today. Cambodia, Laos and East Thailand are now separate mission fields.[3]

The topography is largely a plateau with mountain ranges running from north to south. There are fertile plains in the deep valleys between the mountains, and these are watered by several great rivers and many smaller streams. Located on the plains, and on the west deltas that have been formed at the mouths of the different rivers, are rice fields and other plantations so rich that famine is unknown in that part of the world.[4]

The French Indo-China mission field had been opened up in 1911, and Alliance missionaries had been there for about 12 years. As early as 1882, Dr. Albert B. Simpson, had looked compassionately at the Indo-China peninsula. At that time it was one of the many areas of the world where the Good News of Jesus Christ had yet to be preached. It wasn't until 1911 that R.A. Jaffray, a Canadian and a C&MA Missionary to China, spearheaded the first permanent Protestant incursion into Viet Nam. They entered Tourane, now called Da Nang. R.A. Jaffray himself never established a residence in Viet Nam but he continued to oversee the initial work there. They were looking for new missionaries to expand the missionary front in Indo-China.[5]

In the pamphlet that Dr. Snead gave us to read, an article titled "*LAUNCH OUT*" stirred our hearts. *Through the centuries noble armies of Christian heroes, men,*

*women, and children, have heard the call, and launched
out into the deep: some to far-distant climes, some to
pain, sorrow and suffering, some to glorious martyr-
dom...How often the Christian is like some noble ship
with all canvas set, a strong wind blowing, tugging and
straining at its anchors, eager to launch out on the voyage, - but not able. Oh! May we let go of the things that
hold us back: the sins, pleasures, and desires of this world.*

Our desire was to be a missionary, but just not so far
away. As we backed off, the Lord began to speak to us
in no uncertain terms. They were having revival meetings
at the Institute at that time, but we weren't hearing from
the Lord because we were not fully surrendered to His
calling for us. We thought we were, but we weren't. We
struggled with the thought for several days, but the only
word that stuck in our mind was: Indo-China (Annam)
now known as Viet Nam. Finally, one day when I knew
there was no other way, I just dropped on my knees and
said, "Come on, Mary, we might as well give up; we
know where He wants us to go." So we prayed and cried
before the Lord and He gave us the commitment that has
lasted a lifetime. Praise Him for His great faithfulness!

A Privilege Unique

*There's no angel could ever do
What God has called us to do,*

For they're not made in God's likeness
And never been born anew.

Angels desire to look into
The things the prophets foretold,
They can't grasp Redemption's story
Like, to us it doth unfold.

Created in God's own image
Yet terribly marred by sin,
Jesus identified with us
He came down our hearts to win.

Transformed with the mind of Jesus
That we, our dear Lord might know,
And be filled with His Holy Spirit
And endowed with power to go.

We are weak but He is so strong
His strength, perfect in weakness,
So we go to proclaim His love
Humbly and in all meekness.

The hosts of heaven are amazed
As they see what God can do,
Through His church, the body redeemed
Dungeon and fire they go through.

They no longer count, their lives dear
They go regardless of cost,

To tell what only they can tell
To reach the dying and lost.

At last when the story is told
And Jesus comes back again,
What a throng will welcome that day
His glorious reign will begin.

The angels will bow in silence
While we shout songs of praise,
To Christ our blessed Redeemer
Who works in such marvelous ways.

As far as commitment is concerned, we had no more problems. When we surrendered all, that was it! And something inside us had begun to change. It was in 1923 that we told Dr. Alford Snead, "Okay, we are glad to go to the old land of Annam on the other side of the earth. It's what our dear Lord wants. It is such a privilege, and to go in fellowship with such a precious society as The Christian and Missionary Alliance is so delightful."

5

To Viet Nam

During the summer of 1924, while funds were coming in for our passage to France and Viet Nam, we were appointed for tour in New England to different churches; witnessing, preaching and getting ready. So, off we went again for our last trip in the dear old Model T. They sent us out for the summer here and there, then we were back to Nyack for a final few months.

Finally, word came from the C&MA that we were booked on the biggest steamship in the world, the *Leviathan*, an old war trophy that America had taken from Germany after World War I. We were almost ready to go; we went down town to New York to get our passports and papers in order.

I can remember the thrill when I saw that great big old ship. We boarded that thing March 15, 1925, and headed for France. What a thrill to think we were actually on our way, but oh, what a pull on those heart strings. Off for years, to be away from friends and loved ones, in the midst of strange people with a strange language.

The first part of our trip took us to France where we were to do our language studies. Mary had already had a good course in French in school, and I, the dumbbell, hadn't had anything. I had one lesson of Spanish which certainly didn't make me fluent, and that wasn't of any use anyway. We were in France eight months studying the French language because Viet Nam was a French Colony. The C&MA was urgently in need of missionaries because the field had just opened up after the war and nothing much had happened yet.

We were then off on another steamship, the *d'Artagnan*, loaded with war material, horses, and cannons, because France was having trouble with Beirut at that time. Well, we didn't worry about that, we just got on the ship with two other missionary couples and were on our way. We went out through the Mediterranean Sea, down the Suez Canal, out in the Indian Ocean, all beyond anything we'd ever dreamed of, and past India, Malaysia and Singapore and then into French Indo-China, and up that old winding Saigon River. Finally, in the heat of our first tropical day, we dropped anchor at Saigon on January 16, 1926. Under French rule, Saigon became a modern city with a powerful Vietnamese Roman Catholic elite, but most Vietnamese were Buddhists. Later Saigon would become notorious for government corruption, gambling dens, prostitution, and the opium trade.[1]

I remember stepping off onto that land was such a thrill. When we walked down that dock in the midst of those strange people whom we had never seen before, we could hear the Lord say, "This is for life." We said, "Okay, Lord, we are committed." Every bridge burned, there was no return. That would be our home for the next 50 years. We had made up our minds that we were not going for a short stretch and then coming home and writing our memoirs. That wasn't the idea. We had decided that this was going to be our home for life. There we were in a land where very few people had ever heard the good news of God. How terrible to think that down through the centuries the free, full salvation of our Lord and Saviour had never reached them and The Christian and Missionary Alliance was the only society that had finally come with the GOOD NEWS, which in Vietnamese is *"Tin lành!"*

We had no sooner gotten there when the Mission brought two French cars to use on the field. No one else knew how to drive a car or had a license so I had a job immediately. I also had a lot of mechanical knowledge from working on things. There was just a handful of missionaries on the job at that time, and the chairman, Rev. Edwin F. Irwin, was on a station way up country at a place called Tourane (now named Da Nang) which was where the Alliance first landed in French Indo-China. He had come to Saigon to meet us and the only way for him to get back with one of the new cars was for me to drive, so off we went through hundreds of miles of primitive roads to our destination. When we finally arrived at our destination, I was given the job of auto mechanic because the car was in bad shape and needed some work. After working on the car for a few days, I decided that I didn't come all the way to Viet Nam to be a mechanic, so I turned the job over to some of the nationals who would work on it, and decided to learn the language.

There we settled down in one of the hardest, most bewildering, discouraging tasks ever imagined. Vietnamese is a tonal language with five different tones. A change in tone changes the meaning of the word. It was the strangest thing that a guy with no desire for a language should fall in love with that language. I never fell in love with Latin while in high school, but my dear wife and I fell in love with the Vietnamese language, and I suppose the reason was that we fell in love with the people. That's the secret, and it comes from the Lord as He put the love in our hearts for the poor lost race that had been left out for so long. We both sat down and made our minds up that we were going to learn to speak the language like they do. We completely took ourselves away from the hobnobbing with those people who spoke English.

Generally, on a station like that, missionaries gather and have good times together, and there's nothing wrong with that. But when you spend too much time speaking English with people and preaching in English, you don't learn the language. We more or less isolated ourselves and spent time with the Vietnamese. We found someone who spoke the language correctly and paid him to teach us Vietnamese. That was one long year, six hours a day practicing tones and examining the mouth and throat of one who was not a speech teacher, but only knew how to speak his mother language. That was just a start. We would take turns; one going out among the people, listening to tones, while the other worked with the teacher.

Then in 1927 we had our first field conference for the missionaries; there weren't many there at that time, maybe 20. Dr. A.C. Snead, the field representative was out from New York and handled the meeting. During those days, they appointed different ones to their separate missionary stations throughout the land. All the way from Hanoi, hundreds of miles to the north and hundreds of miles to the south, there was no missionary and there never had been. Central Viet Nam was called a "protectorate" and the French would not allow any religions to be taught there except Buddhism and Catholicism, which were already established there. No other missionary society was working in Viet Nam at the time. Tourane was a French concession and the Gospel was allowed there, but outside that small territory no other religion was allowed.

The conviction grew on us that it was time to challenge the powers of darkness in the name of Jesus. Mary and I had a deep conviction for an area outside of Tourane where they didn't allow any missionary work. There were missionaries further south down in the Delta and Saigon. We felt called to a section of Viet Nam where there was no Gospel message or ray of light, and where no missionaries had been. They were truly "in the dark." It was forbidden territory as there was a decree out by the local officials that allowed no Protestants to preach there.

I told Dr. Snead that Mary and I felt we should go out from this section of the country, not to stay in Tourane or even the Delta where missionaries were already working. We felt we needed to accept the challenge of Central Viet Nam and move down to a place called Nha Trang in the Khanh Hoa province, two or three hundred miles south of Tourane. That's half way between Tourane (which was later called Da Nang) and Saigon.

Dr. Snead knew how deep our convictions were and was impressed by our desire to enter this forbidden territory. He told the others at the conference, "You better listen to that young man." And the Mission did; so if we could get permission from the local officials to go down to Nha Trang to live, then we could do it. We went to the government of that country and got the needed permission and found a place to rent. We were officially appointed to the station of Nha Trang in 1927, far away and alone in a territory that comprised four provinces with at least a million people. We had asked the Mission to let us call their bluff and go anyway, which left everybody wondering how it would turn out. We might get kicked out of the land altogether, but there was the commitment we had made, and the Lord was in it all. With Him "in the boat," all is well. We wanted to go. They had waited too long already and if we got kicked out that would be up to the Lord. "Thou will keep him in perfect peace whose mind is stayed on Thee, because he trusteth in Thee." (Isaiah 26:3)

Go and Tell Them

That Word "Go quickly and tell them"
Greatest word ever announced,
Greater than any news item
Ever from satellite bounced.

They were just two humble women
No credentials had they,
They hurried with that good news
They had the scoop of the day.

The greatest break-through of all time
That resurrection story,
Broke upon a darkened world
That beam of endless glory.

Jesus with infinite power
Over death, hell and the grave,
Says: "Go quickly as possible"
With headlines: "JESUS SAVES."

Nha Trang is on the coast and its beautiful water front makes it an ideal seaside resort town. The city is flanked by nearly ten kilometers or six miles of prime beach where the water is warm year round. It is an area that is praised most because of having a range of mountains framing the beach and makes one think of Hawaii. The bay encircles coral reefs and the sand is a beautiful white. The average temperature in Nha Trang is 26° C (78° F) and the lowest level of humidity in all of Viet Nam. It has long been known to have the best weather in Viet Nam.[2] This was the place we would call home for the next several years.

6

Forbidden Territory

E ven though our language was not yet perfect, we started out to meet the people. We had an old "rattle trap" second-hand Model T Ford again. We loaded it with tracts and Bibles and were on the road most of the time; it was a shaky affair.

Wherever we stopped, the crowds would gather to hear foreigners speaking their language and giving out free tracts and Bibles. Once the officials came rushing over to where we were. They didn't stop, just took note of what we were up to and went on. The next day they called me in and reminded me that any religious propaganda was strictly forbidden. It made little difference what they said; we knew we had orders from a Higher Authority. With all politeness, we just went on quietly and prepared for the next attack on the enemy's territory. It was somewhat scary, but it is better to obey God than man.

There we were the next day, loaded and on the road with that wonderful story of God's love, fully confident that "if God be for us who can be against us?" (Romans 8:31) We always said to the Lord, "If we get thrown out, it will be up to You; we can do nothing but obey."

Along the way we would go and when we'd stop the crowds would gather around. We never saw anything like it in our lives. We would get a grass shed someplace, meet with the people for prayer, and the Vietnamese officials would come in and drag the Vietnamese people off to court and I would follow along and listen. Of course, it was embarrassing to the officials for me to go along and pay attention to what they were doing. In every town, they would slap the Christians around. Mary and I would be on our knees in prayer in some grass hut. They would bang them around and drag them off to the officials and I'd go along. We didn't stop preaching, but just went along the same way as always. We had to believe that the Lord was planning and doing this. So, we just went and preached and for three years that continued. The local officials would threaten us and tell us what would happen to us, but we just completely disobeyed the local officials.

In the different towns we entered, we would open a chapel in a building along the street, get some chairs and a box for the pulpit, and contact the Bible school at Tourane telling them that we needed a preacher. When we got him installed, we would move on to another town or village, planting the "seed" for future churches.

During all this time, our speaking language became more like theirs, which was such a delight.

While we were away for several weeks from the Nha Trang station, which we called home, they put the local preacher in jail. They were putting preachers in jail everywhere. When we arrived back on that station we found him there, not discouraged or complaining but preaching the Gospel in jail. He was going right along with the Christian policy of obeying God rather than man. It was Mr. Lieu, a powerful preacher who had spent many years serving the devil, entertaining people with his sinful acts and speeches. Now he was preaching the Gospel in jail; he had baptized several new believers right there in prison.

In order to share what was happening in our lives on the other side of the world and ask our supporters for prayer, I wrote one of my first missionary updates in October of 1928 from our new station at Nha Trang titled *Hiding – in Annam*:

"Hiding where? 'With Christ in God,' the only place of safety and success. To step out and try to fight this battle in the flesh would be immediate failure, but to hide away and rest in Him Who never lost a battle is a wonderful privilege.

"What shall we do when organized opposition comes in like a flood, when the native preacher is put in prison, and we are absolutely forbidden to further the Gospel by word of mouth or printed page? What shall we do in the face of an official decree such as the following:

PUBLIC NOTICE

According to the decision of the Royal Court, the first month the fourth day of the third year of King Bao-Dai, may it be brought to the remembrance of the people that only Roman Catholics have the right to propagate their religion in this Province of Annam.

All other religions are absolutely forbidden, excepting only the different religions that the Annamese people have followed from of old to the present time, which are their ordinary customs and thus not forbidden.

Thus all superstitious religions are prohibited: Christianity, the Gospel, and Cao-Daiism are all absolutely forbidden.

Whosoever does not obey the above decision shall be punished.

Nha Trang, March 2nd, 1928.

"This notice was posted up on the chapels, in the market places, and heralded throughout all Annam. Christians were threatened and told to burn their Bibles, some hid theirs, others weak and wavering obeyed and burned the precious Book, and others who never professed to follow the Lord were glad for an excuse to get rid of the Book that they had happened to buy. Many hundreds of Bibles and tracts had been distributed, one hundred and fifty persons had professed conversion, and two new out-stations had been opened. But what were these timid souls to do in the face of such opposition?

"This is how things looked after seven months of labor here in Southern Annam. Seven times around the walls of Jericho in seven days and seven times the seventh day, but still the walls stand and they shout from the top of the wall and jeeringly ask, 'When are you going to leave?' Many times we have been told that our 'religion' was forbidden and asked when we were going to leave. Truly it seemed that there was nothing else to do. But thank God, His people are praying, and as we hide away in Him and shout the victory the wall of opposition must fall.

"As a great ocean liner plows majestically through the raging sea in the dark night against the fierce wind and mighty waves, what folly it would be to cast one's self in the water and try to struggle against such overwhelming opposition! No, the only thing to do is to hide away in the cozy little cabin in the bosom of the great ship and ride triumphantly on.

"Our God is moving on with irresistible power. Nothing is hard for Him. He is not struggling here in Annam. He is moving triumphantly on. God forbid that we step out and struggle in the flesh when we have the wonderful privilege of hiding in Him and riding on to victory.

"But you ask what is actually being done? For three or four months after the above decree we gathered with little groups of Christians at Nha Trang and the different outstations for *nothing but prayer*. We did not even dare unite in singing a song in the chapels for fear of being charged with the sin of holding a meeting in direct disobedience to the royal decree.

"It was at one of these prayer meetings that the native preacher, Mr. Lieu, was put in prison. As time went on we began to read the Bible and explain it, then later we would gather with more liberty to sing and praise the Lord and expound the Word. People began to lose their fear and so would buy Gospels and tracts and listen to us explain the way of salvation. Mr. Lieu is still in prison serving a five month sentence for preaching. In the past three months, fourteen prisoners have professed conversion through Mr. Lieu's faithful witnessing for his all-sufficient Saviour. As we have been going to the different towns and villages, twenty-seven souls have been saved in the last three months and two have been baptized, one of these a man completely delivered from the awful opium habit. Victory is assured as God's people continue to pray.

"Please pray that we may be kept 'hidden,' and that these people may see only the Lord moving triumphantly on to the evangelization of this dark land."

We, along with the preachers they sent to fill the opened pulpits, were a basket of "hot potatoes" with whom the officials did not know what to do. We paid little attention to their edicts and threats. Of course, they did not want the word to get out in France about what was happening in their colony, but after three years it finally did. The news of the persecution got back to France and the French officials learned that there was no religious liberty in the French colony and they soon put a stop to it. Then, people who prided themselves that their country stood for freedom of religion put a stop to forbidding the preaching of the Gospel in Annam (now Viet Nam). We praised the Lord and kept right on course.

About this time we felt the need, along with some of the other missionaries, to persuade the Mission to establish a school for our children at that beautiful hill station of Dalat. As I mentioned before, our little girl Evangel was such a blessing and so cheerful, always bringing great joy to the home. She had arrived on the field at age four with us, before any of our boys came along.

The Lord sent two ladies, Mrs. Homer-Dixon and Miss Heikenin to our field who were chosen to open the school. Mrs. Homer-Dixon mothered the first three missionary children, George Irwin (son of the Field Chairman), Harriette Stebbins and our little Evangel Travis. Later when Mrs. Homer-Dixon left for other missionary work, Herbert and Lydia Jackson came in to be dorm parents at the Dalat School. In the beginning a house had to be rented, but soon God raised up the funds to purchase land and a school was built.[1] The school was located next door to a palace where the king's mother lived and was the school we would eventually send each of our children to.

Dalat is located 150 miles north of Saigon and is often bathed in clouds and cooled by mountain breezes. Because of its pleasant temperate climate and the beauty of its surroundings of lakes, waterfalls, and pine forests, it became popular with the French after 1912 as a cool retreat, resort, and recreation center from the heat of the plains of Indochina. Prominent French officials and well-to-do Vietnamese came to rest, swim in the lake, and hunt tigers and elephants in nearby big-game hunting preserves. Dalat became known as "Le Petit Paris."[2]

We had seen little babies weaned, but that was the beginning of weaning days and years for us. It was so painful when we had to take Evangel, at age seven, off to school and leave the home empty. I can remember so well traveling along the roads in Viet Nam, and Mary and I would be so overcome with emotion that we would just hold hands and cry. Those were very difficult days for us when we couldn't help but question our calling to the mission field. We felt blessed that God was so good to give us such a precious girl through the years.

Then after seven years, along came Jonathan Adriel on March 20, 1928 to cheer us up. He was born while we were visiting in Saigon. We went to the hospital in Saigon and then I took over. They figured they couldn't do anything with me and couldn't keep me out, so they turned the whole deal over to me.

Jonathan was so full of life and good mischief which made life so interesting. We were so happy to have our home filled with the love of another little one. We made a bamboo fence to keep him from the floor, where so many bare feet trod during the busy day. It wouldn't take him long to shake it to pieces and get out.

On April 30, 1929, Mary typed the following update letter from Nha Trang, Annam to some of our loved ones back home with news of what we were doing for the Lord, "We are thinking now about getting ready for the Conference. It begins May 19th. We have to leave home three days early so in two weeks we will be going. All the missionaries from the South have to come through Nha Trang so we usually plan to stay till the last ones have passed through. It is nice for them to have a place to stop for a little rest especially the ones with little children. They get awfully tired traveling in the heat.

"This past year has gone very quickly although it has been an extra trying year for us. We feel about ready for a little rest. With no Annamese helpers it has been very hard. But the Lord's strength and grace has been sufficient. Then to send little Evangel away to school just about taxed my strength to the limit. Praise God there is victory in Jesus and peace and joy that the world knows nothing about. I know in our own strength we would have failed a hundred times over but Jesus, He has never failed yet, and He never will.

"Last week we made a three day trip into the country. We stayed in a Chinese hotel at night and had a woman along who kept Jonathan at the hotel through the day. We surely had a good time. Where we have no established work, we just ride or walk along and witness to those we meet. Many are very eager to listen, buy books and want to hear more, and some are careless and seemingly satisfied to worship their ancestors and idols. But we know in their hearts there is no rest. They just follow the customs handed down to them by their forefathers without knowing why.

"We stopped by the roadside under a huge tree that is held sacred by the natives and cooked Jonathan's food. Under this tree there was a little house of worship erected on four poles. Inside this little house there were all the articles of worship, incense sticks, rice bowls, little idols, etc. The poor deluded people come here, offer their food to their unseen gods and worship. We opened the door, aired the place out, and put the little gas stove inside so that it might be protected from the wind and boiled some water to fix the baby's food. The Annamese would think that they would surely be cursed to use this holy place in this way. They fear their gods. Most of their worship is done out of fear. They do it that they may ward off some great evil. Most of the Annamese believe that there is a Great Spirit (Ong Troi) who is the god of the heavens. But it is very strange that they never think of worshipping him. It is always the devil or the demons, whom they thoroughly believe in, that they worship. They do it so that the devil and demons will not disturb them."

Once we were home from conference we went back to preaching out in the countryside and holding open-air meetings. Everywhere we stopped along the road we got out and preached. We had no P.A. system at that time. That would come later. We just got up on a soap box and preached. Everybody knew we were doing the right thing. The officials that were opposing us and threatening us didn't want anything to do with us. Satan and the Vietnamese government itself didn't want it, but we went ahead and folks were saved.

We'd open a little chapel or "hole in the wall" anywhere. We'd go into a town where they had never heard the gospel and find a place we could rent and get some chairs and a pulpit and get up and preach. We were such curiosities. The Vietnamese people never heard a Frenchman preach the Vietnamese language like that. But here we were Americans speaking in their language.

For us to come in and begin to tell about that wonderful Gospel story, how Jesus came and giving all the details; it was just wonderful.

We were always out on the road for *one* purpose, and that was to reach the lost for the Lord. As soon as we'd get a group in any town or anyplace, they would soon find a place to assemble, rent a place, and later build a church. As it happened throughout the 50 years, there must have been 30 or more churches built. As the Vietnamese would begin to gather a large congregation, they would build themselves a church. Of course, the Americans helped a lot. We built 12 churches in that one province. That was our business right down through the years. We had a wonderful experience to be able to go to those people!

We were down in Saigon a year and a half later on November 1st of 1929, when our next little boy, Ivan Earl, came along. He got his nick-name Ike when Jonathan was learning to talk. He couldn't say Ivan; he would say "Ikie." So, the name Ike stuck through the years.

I remember so well when Ike was just a baby. Babies didn't stop us from those evangelistic trips. This time, at a place called Phan Thiet, we were having regular meetings every evening, and during the day we'd be out visiting with the people. We had a trustworthy young girl along with us to take care of Jonathan and Ike. One day we were on our way visiting, and to get to the homes we wanted to visit, we had to cross the river. There was no bridge so the only way was by canoe—the tide was out and the river low, so to get to the boat we had to walk on logs that were laid deep in mud along the river bank. The girl was carrying Ike across a slippery water soaked log. All at once she slipped and fell, dropping Ike in the deep soft mud. How good that it was mud instead of hard ground! We picked him up, completely covered with thick black mud.

Whenever we had one or more of the children along, it was always an amazing attraction to the Vietnamese. They would gather around gazing at a little white baby, something they had never seen before. What an opportunity to tell them how Jesus came as a baby! It always made a lasting impression on the people and was such a wonderful means of reaching into their lives and pointing them to Jesus.

7

A Missionary's Wife

" And the LORD God said, 'It is not good that the man should be alone; I will make him an help meet for him.' " (Genesis 2:18) What a help-meet the Lord gave me! Mary surely did help meet the spiritual needs of the Vietnamese women. She wasn't out there just as a missionary's wife, *she was a mission-ary*. She was out to touch the hearts of those women. If you reached the woman in the home, you got the home, because she's the boss, even though the man is the figurehead and thinks he's boss. She holds the pock-etbook; she does the marketing; she takes care of the children and plans the day and the meals. The man also works, but in Vietnamese culture it is crucial to reach the women, as these women were steeped in fetishes and ancestor altars, which take up one third of the lit-tle hut they live in. If you go in their village, and some-body doesn't reach those women, even though the man consents to accept Jesus, he doesn't last unless the wife comes through too, so to speak. Otherwise, they are both back to worshipping at the ancestor altar as they did before.

Very few people in the Western World understand how it works or what this altar is all about. The altar is where they believe that their ancestors come back to visit. The ancestor altar is usually a table in the main entrance of the house, which is decked out as elaborately as possible according to their financial ability. On the customary red tablecloth are candles, incense, different gods represented by words written in character, and many pictures of ancestors. There the family members come on different occasions to bow. I don't like to use the word "worship" because there's no such thing as worship in the heathen religion. It's only to appease the spirits of the departed dead, or that was the practice anyway. That's all there was to it, but very few people understand it. Even the Vietnamese people themselves don't understand until you explain it. And to think of a foreigner going out there explaining it to them is something they never dreamed of. When the departing of the spirit of the person who dies takes place, they immediately believe he becomes an evil spirit and can come back and cause trouble, even death, if the spirit is not appeased. So, they "worship," appeasing evil spirits, which is from the pit of the devil himself.

We'd go into the hut and sit down and explain the Gospel to them and they'd agree with everything we'd

8

Always an Adventure

It's so good to be committed to the One who is able to handle every situation. So from 1925 to 1931, we had completed the first stage in the best days of our lives.

I must say a few words about this first furlough. Because there were no planes in those days, we were booked to leave Hong Kong on a Canadian steamer but our third little boy, Paul, was about to arrive. He was late and we had to cancel that first booking and try to make the next Canadian liner, the *Empress of Russia*.

Then came Paul. The little careless kid finally arrived 16 days later on April 7, 1931 while we were still at our station in Nha Trang. I can remember when I was going to register him as an American while in Saigon. We had decided to call him Paul Adrian, but Mary called to me as I was leaving for the French office and said, "I am afraid if we call him Paul Adrian they will nickname him Pat." "Okay," I said, "we'll call him Adrian Paul," but in later years he called himself Paul.

We wired the folks in Tourane, "Rushing for the *Russia*." It surely was a rush for me from that moment on, storing our earthly belongings and taking care of four children as well as my dear wife, who was not "back in the harness." The Lord gave strength for each day and those where hectic days!

We arrived in Saigon just as the head of the bank in Saigon had died and there was no one else around to conduct the funeral except me. I had to change from work clothes to more appropriate garb for that funeral. However, we were soon on a French ship headed for Hong Kong, where there was another delay waiting for the *S.S. Russia* to leave for America. Lots of thrills, as I later had time to think about it, but I had my hands full with four children - two of them toddlers and an infant - and a recuperating wife. Finally the *Russia* rushed into Hong Kong harbor and we were on board. They gave us two cabins; one I turned into a wash and laundry room. Luvs and Pampers had not arrived in those days, so you can imagine how it was in those good old days, just ordinary cloth diapers and safety pins. It was good that I was only thirty-three years old and never knew what it was to be tired, so, come what may, I did not seem to mind.

We landed in Vancouver, Canada, but still far from Maine, our destination. We boarded a tourist train of the Canadian Pacific Railroad and were off clear across Canada with still new experiences. On this train with low-rate fares, we had to take care of ourselves. Seats were turned into beds at night and I had to do the turning. As far as eating was concerned, I was chief cook and bottle washer and there were plenty of other things to wash besides bottles, still no Pampers! As the train stopped at stations along the way, I rushed out to some nearby store, grabbed an arm load of victuals and made it back to the train before they left me. Other times when they stopped, I would see a stream of water and would run with a bucket of diapers that needed processing. So, on it went for days across beautiful Canada, but I had little time to view its beauty.

As we neared Montreal, I learned that in West Montreal there was a branch railroad that went directly down to Maine Central Railroad. But all our baggage was locked and sealed in the baggage car and destined for Montreal. Unless something could be done, we would land in Montreal with no place to go and the task of getting back to that Maine Central Railroad Station. I contacted the conductor and for hours they had to negotiate with the authorities for permission to unlock that baggage car and let me in to find our baggage and get it piled near the door, ready to dump during the brief stop at West Montreal. They finally got permission and at the next stop, they locked me in that baggage car. It was stacked to the ceiling with hundreds of pieces of baggage belonging to all the passengers on that long train.

What a hopeless task to find our bags way back in the corner down under such a mess of trunks and suitcases. With youthful strength I was finally able to find each piece and wrestle it over near the door to be dumped at the Maine Central Station in West Montreal. Arriving there, they unlocked the car and out I rolled with all the baggage. Then along came my wife and four children, whom I had not been able to care for during that night. We all sat as the train pulled out and left us sitting on that pile of baggage, waiting for the train to Maine. Soon the old steam engine with the necessary cars pulled in and we were on the last lap of our journey. What a reunion with Mary's folks in Fryeburg, Maine! After so many years, the thrill was overwhelming, with praise and thanksgiving for God's faithful keeping through the years.

9

Church Planting

We had come home for furlough and figured it was about time to "come apart" for a little so we wouldn't really come apart. There are three reasons for furlough: time for much needed rest and a little change, time to see friends and loved ones we had not seen for years, and last, but not least, time to meet the people who had been praying and giving, making it possible for missionaries to be out there with this glorious Gospel. This was done by missionary conventions all over the country. Our tours sometimes lasted for three months or more.

Someone would ask, "Now haven't you done enough? You have opened the way; can't you let someone else carry on from here?" Oh no. It's for life. They are our people; it's for life, not just a temporary adventure; we are committed. How can we stay home when there are still millions who have never heard? That year passed quickly and back again we went on the most thrilling adventure I've known. What joy to be able to join the greatest rescue parties in all the world! How rewarding to see the happy faces delivered from the bondage of Satan, in congregations praising the Lord with songs sung from the bottom of their hearts.

To The Rescue

The storm is on o'er all the earth
And sin is taking its toll,
Disaster is rampant everywhere
As the powers of evil roll.

We should hasten to the rescue
And obey the Lord's command,
As we tell forth the word of life
To the lost in every land.

Christ Jesus died that they might live
And He has told us to go,
Preach the gospel to everyone
That all the world may know.
To neglect this great salvation
And not tell it everywhere,
Is a crime that's called: "Soul Murder"
That should set our hearts astir.

So "sin is lying at the door"
And it's a horrible thing,
If we don't hasten with the Word
And God's great deliverance bring.

While this emergency is on
Think not of ease or pleasure,
Let the love of Christ constrain us
Each rescue is our treasure.

Treasures laid up there in heaven
That will last forevermore,
And they'll join with us in worship
Over on that peaceful shore.

Time is short, redeem it NOW
Never again will there be,
A chance to serve our Lord like this
Throughout all eternity.

In spite of all the toil, tears and war through the years, would we have wanted it any other way? Things were not just about to happen; they did happen, and I will try to tell more of the years following 1931. In looking back, it all seems like a dream. How could it ever be? But, Jesus makes things real and everlasting!

We returned in 1932, this time across the Pacific Ocean taking a Model A Ford (to replace the old worn out Model T), to run the roads and trails of Viet Nam. By that time we had accumulated the three boys (Jonathan, Ivan, and Paul), besides our daughter, Evangel, who had to live in their midst and put up with them.

Once back from furlough we were back to our

routine of preaching and visiting the people. We took Evangel back to school in Dalat. During the war, the city of Dalat was considered to be a neutral zone and was spared fighting and destruction. Of course, that made for more heartaches and pain as the children had to be away from home nine months out of the year.

Our field conferences were always held in Dalat so at conference time we were able to get together, and the children would be home for Christmas and the summer. We hated to have to leave them at school. Our oldest son Jonathan grieved a lot when we left him the first time, but he soon fit in. They all got along. The Lord comforted the children as He comforted us parents. We always made such a point to hurry and pick them up for vacations. "All things work together for good to them that love the Lord, to them who are called according to His purpose." (Romans 8:28) The main thing was loving the Lord; then, however things work out, it will be good anyway no matter how tough the going is. Having absolute faith in the Lord's guidance, I knew that everything that would happen had a purpose and it was all for good.

What happened during the years before they began to go off to school at Dalat? The children went right along on all the trips of preaching and planting churches. In those early years we didn't have any set way to visit a village; we'd just go in and find an empty place to live. When entering a town, we would find some kind of a building—no matter what, clean the place and move in for the duration. We never knew how long we were to stay any more than the children of Israel did before moving on. That made no difference as long as we had the cloud by day and the pillar by night. The same God guides today. He is the same yesterday, today, and forever! (Hebrews 13:8)

We preached every night, standing on a soap box or a chair in the open air as the crowds would stand or sit around on the ground and listen. In those early days there was no other attraction. They had nothing to read, there was no radio or TV. Any excitement in the town, like our coming and starting a meeting, would cause the whole town to gather. We'd rent a place and it would be so full there was no more room. There were more people outside trying to get in than there were people inside while we preached the glorious Gospel.

We always tried to have a national preacher along who would witness and preach. After the national preacher spoke, my wife, and I would finish presenting the Gospel to the people. The evening had just begun, and the people were not ready to leave. They gathered around in groups, my wife with the women, the preacher with a crowd in one spot, and me with a crowd of inquirers in another spot. They would begin with all kinds of questions and we knew we must answer them all. Jesus has the answers which we shared with them as long as they stayed. All the time we are pressing for an immediate decision to accept the Lord Jesus and be delivered from Satan's power. Speaking of Satan's power in this far-off land where he has held sway so long is a fearful thing. How we needed the whole armor of God to even dare enter that territory and attempt to take men and women alive! "And others save with fear, pulling them out of the fire..." Jude 23, or literally translated, snatching them as brands from the fire meaning to save them from an eternal death in hell. We were committed and that was the thing we wanted to do. We obeyed God and turned our backs on Satan and all his fearful threats.

This is the way we started in church planting, for many were ready to accept Jesus and wanted to know more. After a night of preaching and witnessing, the next day we were up taking care of our children. What happened to them during the day? We always had a good trusty guy along for that purpose; a fellow who loved the Lord and loved our children. They were in safe hands. During the day we would be on bicycles going from house to house, hut to hut, with the Good News. Many had heard us the night before and were eager to hear more and ask all kinds of questions. Mary would be off with the women as they crowded around to hear her speak that beautiful language telling the most wonderful story ever known. As I said earlier, reaching the women was so important in Viet Nam. They raise the children, do the marketing, plant the rice, a spear at a time, knee deep in water. They also harvest the rice. After it is beaten out by hand they grind it at the mill, which takes the hull off from the rice and leaves them their staff of life. The men plow the field and prepare it for the transplanting of the rice from mud beds where it has been sown. In the midst of their work they are always ready to stop and listen as we arrive with something "new under the sun." They are such hospitable people. They would invite us into their little grass huts and were always ready to hear what we had to say.

They know there is a God in heaven, His name is Duc Chua Troi, the great Lord of Heaven. They never heard that He visited us in human form, revealing Himself to man. They say there has to be a Number ONE. They know there is One who did it, so that is a good starting place as we lead right up to the Best News that ever struck this old sin-cursed world. "How come we never heard of this before?" they would ask us. As we tell the story of how Jesus, the God of heaven, came to earth, things would begin to click. It had the ring of truth. It reached right into where they live. It is just the way it should be, but they had never heard it before. The door would begin to open but, oh, so many adversaries! Satan and his gang are on the job and we fight not against flesh and blood, but against sin, the love of darkness rather than light, and heart depravity. There is such a danger of being presumptuous. We need constant, humble dependence on the only One who said, "All power is given unto Me; go ye, therefore, into all the world and preach the Gospel, and Lo, I am with you always..." (Matthew 28:20) We learned to let the Word which is quick and powerful penetrate the heart, and be quiet in silent prayer as the Spirit of the living God started to break the stony heart.

Our main goal was to establish a church right there in that place so that when we left there would be a place for them to gather. A preacher would be sent from the Bible school in Da Nang (Tourane as it was called then) to take over. We went on to other towns. We'd go north when the rainy season was in the south and go south when the rainy season was in the north.

Everywhere Preaching

In those days of persecution
They were scattered far and wide,
And were sure of one thing only
Jesus Christ was at their side.

They went everywhere a-preaching
Everyone so loved the Lord,
He, their satisfied portion,
Their exceeding Great Reward.

Earthly riches, they had nothing
Neither had they scrip nor purse,

Yet the resurrection story
They must everywhere rehearse.

Trusting in their glorious Saviour
With such power they preached the Word,
So that people came presenting
As their sinful hearts were stirred.

In these days of sin and weakness
It's revival that we need.
Dear Lord, lay Thy hand upon us
For deliverance we plead.

Not by might or any power
But His Spirit from on high,
Will release the poor lost sinners
Blood redemption brings Him nigh.

Yes, the precious blood of Jesus
Poured out there on Calvry's cross,
Is the message God has given
And all else is so much dross.

Thus with resurrection power
All the world will know the way,
For this message straight from heaven
We'll be preaching every day.

10

Family and Work

(1932)

We had a harrowing albeit exciting experience in the southern section of that district. It occurred when all the children were home from school, when we continued our work of visiting the churches. We had to spend several weeks in special meetings with the different churches, and since the rainy season was coming, we decided to go home for Christmas. We heard that the main road home was out because of high water and a bridge was destroyed. The only way to get back was a long detour by way of Dalat, the hill station. We made it that way, but when we got back to the main road to Nha Trang, our home town, they told us the rain was pouring down and roads were flooded. Still I thought we could make it.

It was late in the afternoon, but we hit the road, not realizing what was ahead. Water was everywhere, but we could see the road, and, as long as I could keep the old Ford on the road, all was okay. It soon became like a great lake and the road was fast disappearing. When you can't see the road any more, how can you stay on it? Besides the children, we had a trusty helper along. The only way we could make it was have our helper wade down the water-covered road and stand at a point which I could steer for and not miss the way. We continued that way for perhaps an hour and finally he was too afraid. He said there are tigers in this part of the country. I tried without a guidepost. That was almost impossible, and it proved so within a few miles. On a curve I missed the road. There we were in the midst of pouring down rain with the car about to turn over into ten feet of water beside the road. We all climbed out before we got trapped inside the car in the rushing water. I had a trunk full of materials on the back of the car which I wanted to save. After getting the "gang" out of the car and in about three feet of water on the road, I tied that old trunk to a tree near at hand and with the family, "abandoned ship" for what we hoped might be higher ground down the road.

Can you imagine such a situation: four children along and one had just come down with a case of dysentery which was the main reason we were hurrying home. As it was, we weren't hurrying home very fast. After wading in water, hip deep for about 100 yards, we came to a bridge which was a little higher, so we were afforded a place for a little rest and a prayer meeting. It is certain we asked the Lord for help; we were far from home with no way to get there. It was dark, but we had left the lights on in the half-submerged car so we could see, but a turn in the road deprived us of that help. On we went, feeling our way, hoping to soon find higher ground. When we did, we sat down in some bushes beside the road, too exhausted to go any further. As we prayed in the dark, we saw a light over in the field. By the lightning flashing from time to time, we could see that there was much water between us and a little grass hut, the source of the light. We yelled to the occupants to please show us how to get to the house and the shelter it would afford us poor creatures. What a situation: Americans out in the rain with no place to go, begging for help from a poor Vietnamese family.

They came to our rescue, directing us to their little house. What kind hospitality! It was cold rain, coming down from the mountains all around; we were soaked. The man ripped off a bamboo door from a shed outside and made a fire to dry us. They had no place for us to rest except some hard board benches that were too short for us. We stretched out on the boards. It was soon morning. To our great joy, the sun began to shine on us.

After some hot rice they prepared for us, I was on my way back to see if the old Ford was still there. It was still clinging to the bank and had not turned over. By this time, folks had appeared to help heave the old car out of the ditch and back on the road. Water had filled the gear box and the grease had seeped out all over everything. I had no idea if I would ever get the old water-soaked car started. I stepped on the starter and, to my amazement, it started. Down the road I went. Mary and the children were out praising the Lord that we had a way to get home. We did not leave until we had a good meeting in the morning sunshine. You see, the Lord timed things right so that those people would hear about Jesus. He took care of them as well as us.

Two or three of the little children had worn caps in the rain which were lined with red cloth bands. The red dye had faded and left red bands around their heads and across their foreheads. In talking to the people, I used that to illustrate the blood of Jesus, the covering for our sins. What a joy to be giving forth the Words of Life in season and out of season, regardless of the weather, and in such far off regions of the earth. Praise the Lord! After about 75 miles more, we reached home. We spent a week or two recuperating before taking the children off to school, and then once again set off on the trail with the wonderful Words of Life.

11

Camping for Christ

On August 23rd of 1934 while in Nha Trang, we had the final addition to our family, another little boy named Urban Vaughn. That made a complete team. The ocean trips on furlough with that bunch had some headaches, if you want to call it that, trying to keep them from going overboard. When you have four rowdies like that running all over the place, I'll tell you right now, you have to watch them all the time.

Poor Evangel had a tough time with those four guys. Little hoodlums running around having fun, and getting into mischief but I thought they never did anything wrong. They were perfect. We didn't have to spank them much. Not much trouble along those lines. The main thing is they had to tell the truth. There were accidents and that was no problem, breaking things or doing things like that was never a worry. There wasn't much punishment for that. But to deliberately tell a lie, then they were in trouble. The only way they could ever get out of it was to tell the truth, own up, confess and get right. In the meantime, they could be pardoned by the "governor." They knew it didn't pay to tell any lies.

Another area where we were very strict was how they treated others. They were not allowed to mistreat the Vietnamese children. Some missionary children felt so cocky, above the other children—the Vietnamese—pushing them around and mistreating them. That didn't go in our place, no sir. Boy, if they did anything like that, they would have to apologize and get straightened out right off the bat. It made an impression on the people that we respected them and made our children respect them, too. Our ministry was to reach out to the people and our children were part of that ministry.

That same year that Urban was born something new was added, a camp trailer to pull behind the Model A Ford. We found pieces of the old Model T, which we had worn out during our first term, and used the back wheels and the frame and universal joint for hitching because they didn't have trailer hitches in those days. I built the first camp trailer they had seen in that land. I made a steel frame and covered it with slats arranged into louvers allowing for the full flow of air all around, then a double top for circulation of air, (forming its own shade), so we could live in it, eat in it and sleep in it. Rolled canvas was used to keep out the driving rain. We had created a very special means of camping in the midst of the people in faraway places. Trailers were little known in

America at that time and not known at all in Viet Nam. This was ideal for camping in the hot sun of Viet Nam.

There was room inside the six-foot square trailer for two upper and lower bunks, a table for two, and two places to sit. Cooking had to be done outside on the ground under a canvas awning. It was good to pull into a village, find an open space, set up camp in just a few minutes and be ready for business. Paul and Urban were not yet off to school at Dalat. They had a place to sleep and play under the faithful care of our helper, a good Vietnamese Christian, who was so glad to be along serving the Lord. This was our way of living with the people in those distant towns and villages for many years. Such a strange outfit was a wonderful attraction and that is what we wanted, so we could tell everybody about our Lord Jesus. We did not stay in the trailer. We had bicycles, and leaving the children with that faithful helper, we would be off throughout the day telling the whole district of God's love story. The little boys had spent the day playing with home-made toys and cutting up Sears Roebuck catalogues until suppertime. As night came they would crawl back into the bunk beds and go to sleep.

(1935)

Vacation was over and it was time for our three oldest children to return to school in Dalat. On the way back to Dalat, we spent two weeks with one of the preachers in a place called Phan Rang. The twin cities of Thap Cham and Phan Rang are located midway between *Nha Trang* and *Phan Thiet*. The main attraction is a group of Cham towers called Po Klong Garai. The towers were originally built as Hindu temples in the 13th century. They are quite well preserved and offer a good insight into the construction techniques used by the Cham. The site contains several statues and carvings of Hindu gods.

The Cham people are an ethnic group living in Viet Nam, they are considered to be of Malay ethnic stock. Their language belongs to the *Malayo-Polynesian* family and is thus similar to *Malay* and *Indonesian*. We would be the first missionaries to reach these Cham people but that's getting ahead of our story.

We had such a good time during our stay there, preaching every night with many turning to the Lord. The trailer and all our equipment was in an open field close to the church. My wife and I slept in a tent by the trailer so the children could sleep in the trailer. The rain held off during the time of our meeting, but that night it began to rain. We were tired and sleeping soundly in the tent when "visitors" snuck in. Under a canvas shelter we had trunks of children's clothing, new shoes for school, and plenty of needed accessories for the meetings. About two o'clock I was awakened by the sound of the trunk lid slamming shut. I leaped from my tent bunk just in time to see them escaping in the rain with everything that was loose in the tent. The children's clothes, new shoes for school, everything was gone. In the tropical heat I usually slept in a pair of boxer shorts.

Well there we were in pouring down rain with no clothes and everything gone and the car and trailer fast sinking in the mud. I wanted to let the government officials know so they might help in recovering at least some of the equipment and clothing, but how could I run around town in nothing but a pair of boxer shorts? They would then feel certain that I was crazy. Nevertheless, I had to do something. I quickly explained to the officials why I was non-attired so I would not get thrown in the nut house! The outcome? All those earthly goods had evaporated and there was nothing to do but get out of the mud, back on the road, and head for home for a new supply of earthly goods.

Getting out of that deep mud was the problem. It took hours of digging to get that rig out. I didn't need to worry about getting mud on my clothes for I didn't have any, and covering my boxer shorts, I was now "clothed" in a dark colored suit of smooth, shiny mud. The crowd had seen me preaching during the past weeks, but now they stood amazed as they saw a dignified American now "terra"fied by the help of mother earth. After many hours we got the car and trailer on the road ready to return home. We did not hurry. The crowd had increased watching the show, puzzled at what had happened. They thought by that time we should be raving mad at such circumstances, but with the quiet sense of humility we used the situation as an object lesson to tell of the cleansing that comes from Calvary.

As the crowd watched, I walked over to a nearby well, and began to pour gallons of water over my body so covered with mud. Just like magic, I soon was perfectly clean. They had heard me preach during the previous weeks, but no sermon like that. What an illustration and they understood! They asked, "Where are you going?" We said, "Going home to get some clothes." Another illustration: clothed upon with the righteousness of Jesus. Cleaned up and clothed. What a wonderful salvation and what an opportunity to proclaim it to all those people who saw the good news in action. They wishfully asked, "Are you coming back?" We said, "Sure, we'll be back." McArthur said that a few years later when he left the Philippines during World War II. We had a reason to return far greater than any conquering armies of the world. So after a new supply and taking the children to school we were back there again, with a stage all set for a glorious campaign right in the heart of the devil's territory, snatching them as "brands from the burning." Hallelujah!

Reach Them Where They Are

Let's reach the people where they are;
They're waiting in despair,
Let's tell them of God's wondrous grace;
His loving kindness share.

They have no strength to lift themselves
To come to us or pray,
To go with love and God's own Word
Is His appointed way.

In highways and all byways
Our Lord has said to go,
In the power of His own Spirit
His tender mercy show.

With His love and deep compassion
Let's sow the precious seed,
Watered with the tears of mercy,
As we see their direst need.

He has said we'll reap a harvest,
Treasures for our Lord above;
And throughout the endless ages
We will glory in His love.

12

Back Again

Oh, I just happened to remember about a little breakfast mirth when we revisited the town of Phan Rang. It had poured down rain in the night and the nearby river was overflowing its banks. My dear wife was in this little makeshift outdoor bath house taking a bath. We saw the water coming. We thought it was harmless, but as we stood on the back steps, the water kept rising, covering the little platform where the flimsy bath house stood. All at once a surge of water swept by, taking the bamboo bath house with it. My wife stood there knee deep in water. As the structure was leaving, she barely managed to grab enough clothes to cover herself with. The crowd stood there dying with laughter. So there is fun in the floods along the way and in the midst of a jovial people. The real joy is when the Lord takes over with floods of grace and the infinite blessings of His great Salvation.

The Lord was always so good, furnishing rice, pigs, or chicken, and vegetables. We brought them to our camp spot and, with a little clay pot and charcoal, prepared a hot meal. We learned to drink tea and warm water. Refrigerators are not necessary to survive. One day while visiting folks in the village my wife was talking to the women out back. I met the old Grandpa in the house standing before the ancestor altar. He soon found out what I was up to and he had a lot of ideas of his own. This old philosopher who had been around for seventy summers, knew there was a God of the heavens, but thought He was so far away there was no way of making contact with Him. I began telling him that there was a way. "Oh well," he said, "I do worship that God. Once a year I take a bouquet of flowers and I go out under the sky and offer them to that great God." It reminded me of the futility of Cain bringing the fruit of the field as an offering, knowing nothing of God's way through the blood of Jesus, the only way for sinners.

He admitted that was all he knew. I asked him if he really wanted to know God, if he really wanted God to speak to him. He had no idea how. I said, "If you will get on your knees with me right here, you will hear God speak to you and you will know Him." We got on our knees on that dirt floor as I opened the Bible and read, "Though your sins be as scarlet they shall be as white as snow; though they be red like crimson they shall be as wool." (Isaiah 1:18) I said, "The God you offer flowers to loves you so much that He came down to this old earth and took your place on a cross. Flowers could not pay your sin debt, only the blood of the One who came. God became as man to make a way for us to know Him, and we have come to tell you and everybody that He wants to save you." He listened as I told him the whole story of redemption and he drank it in like a little child, ready to accept the most wonderful news he had ever heard. Right then the Spirit of the living God planted the truth in his heart, delivering him from all the darkness that covered his life through all those years.

After a few more days in this place, instructing the ones who had accepted Jesus on how to meet together for prayer and fellowship, we broke camp and started south. One big reason for going south was that the rainy season was coming soon, but in the south we would find different weather. In such a vast territory we could choose the weather needed for continued open-air evangelism. There were always new thrills and spills and this particular trip was no exception.

We traveled along with Paul, Urb, and our faithful helper in the back seat. All of the sudden there was a bang. The war days had not arrived yet, so it wasn't a gun. The left back tire blew and the car began to swerve and skid. Since we were moving quite fast downhill, with the trailer on behind, it looked like we had had it. One final swerve was too much. The trailer turned completely over in the ditch. But the trailer hitch, which was the universal joint of the Model T, did not let loose. It was so good that I had been able to keep the car on the road and upright. What a mess there was in that trailer lying in the ditch with everything inside "homogenized!" With the car pulling and others pushing, we finally got the old crate back on the road and to our surprise, there was very little damage. It was still attached to the car and ready to go. After about an hour's delay, we were on the way again, praising the Lord for a new experience and that we still had the trailer and could travel.

The Overflowing Cup

Fill my cup to overflowing
So that others may receive,
Living waters from the fountain
And their famished souls relieve.

With no overflow from Jesus
Stagnant waters there will be,
Just a selfish soul and useless
Throughout all eternity.

If my cup's not running over
I'll refresh no other soul,
I'll live in isolation
While the endless ages roll.

Though my cup is very little
It can overflow with joy,
As the Lord pours out His blessing
And my weakness He'll employ.

O dear Lord, in Thy great mercy
Let the living waters flow,
Fill my cup to overflowing
That the world Your love may know.

This time we went a long ways south, leaving the Phu Yen Province in the rain and beyond our home base for the sunshine in the Ninh Thuan Province. In 1928 we had first passed through that town and had always wanted to get back there to stay long enough to plant a church. At last the time had come to enter in and take men, women and children "alive" from the enemy of our souls. It was a town where the industry was the making of Vietnamese fish sauce. You can smell the town long before you get there. Some call the smell good; others say it is bad. I soon learned to enjoy the odor and on steaming rice the sauce is so good.

We soon found a "hole in the wall," so to speak, moved in some chairs and a bench, then began preaching. Every night the crowds came. When the place was full, eager listeners would stand in the street trying to catch every word we were saying. They were hearing something they had never heard before and were anxious to get in to inquire more diligently about the Way. What a delight to stay all hours of the night telling poor lost sinners about Jesus!

It soon became evident that God was working in a special way in that town. Every night people flocked to hear the wonderful news. Many did not hesitate to accept Jesus as their personal Saviour. In a few days they brought others and were ready to establish their own place of worship. One particular man had a big *nuoc mam* factory with huge vats of that briny fish sauce, a Vietnamese sauce which is the seasoning of choice for most dishes.[1] His thoughts were now turned to organizing and building a church. So it was that in a short time a church was planted and growing in that dark corner of the earth.

During the weeks of our stay in Phan Thiet, we found a place to bunk which was in the attic of the place where we had been preaching. Of course, we had to go on to other places just as needy as Phan Thiet. So we would be gone for several months before we could return, but when we did, what a surprise! They had their new church built and were rejoicing in the Lord.

What a light house after all those preceding centuries! In our stay this time, we had meetings every night as the crowds came. One night a young man came who had followed Buddhism for many years, but he was still unhappy, spiritually hungry, and looking for something or someone to satisfy his aching heart. He had wandered from temple to temple to no avail. One night as he was passing the church, I was preaching and the right words came out at the right time. This is what he heard, "The Blood of Jesus Christ cleanses from all sin." He stopped right there. What a glorious announcement, taken straight to his heart by the Holy Spirit! He dared to come in to argue for a while, but after all his questions and arguments were answered, he knelt down and joyfully accepted Jesus as his personal Saviour. He never had heard any thing like that in all his life! All his zeal for Buddha turned to Jesus, Who so satisfied his soul that he turned everything over to Him.

He was so anxious to know more that soon he was off to Bible school, studying to minister this wonderful message of Jesus to others. He had come out from Buddhism with such love in his heart for Jesus and his people that no one could resist his testimony. He was so humble, yet with the Word that is quick and powerful, he won people to Jesus everywhere he went. After finishing Bible school he became pastor of the Phan Thiet church and ministered there for several years.

On another trip I had my first and last case of malaria and dysentery. We still had the trailer and the old Model A Ford. I became so weak I couldn't stand and preach, so I had to sit in a chair. I stayed night after night, Mary finally said, "I've got to take you home."

Think of her driving that old Model A Ford and that trailer with me bedded down in the trailer. She got some inner tubes and pumped them up and laid them on the floor of the trailer where I rested. I finally got the car started for her and she braved the trip. She took that thing 150 miles, in the southern part. My wife had never driven our car with the trailer behind it. She wouldn't know if the thing was weaving or twisting or ready to upset. I ran a string from her arm back to where I was so I could give her a jerk once in a while to slow down or take it easy. She was in a hurry to get home with me. We finally landed home. I had such a terrible case of malaria. I must have become immune because I never had it again. We were home for a while recuperating and then set off again up to the north.

We had a district that was 200-300 miles long. Four provinces, each with nearly a million people, and there were no other missionaries in the whole section. Not one. Kind of a large parish for a little twerp like me. Until 1958 we were the only missionaries in that district. Of course, as time went on, we had lots of help from national preachers because we'd get churches established and tell them we needed a preacher.

Planting churches was the main work until finally each province would have one or two or three churches. They came from all over the country for Bible school. When places were available and as new churches opened up, preachers would be appointed and we'd get them in their job as soon as possible. I never pastored a church in Viet Nam. I worked at outdoor evangelism and the churches were pastored by national preachers. We would go for special meetings, but they ran the church. They'd always invite us to come, preach, and carry on meetings. Then we always turned it over to them. That was the whole purpose. No foreign missionary pastored a church out there.

In reading the Book of Acts, one cannot help but notice that each church began with a key man or woman whom the Holy Spirit brought into contact with the apostle. Such were saved and became the nuclei around whom the churches were formed. They were men and women who commanded respect in the community and who were prepared by God to be leaders in the churches. Such were the Ethiopian eunuch; Barnabas the Levite; Cornelius the centurion; Saul of Tarsus; Lydia the seller of purple; Apollos; Aquilia and Priscilla; the jailer at Philippi, and many more. The Lord works in the same way today.[2]

13

The Cham People

It was in this section of our district that we had such happy experiences. We went everywhere preaching. By that time we had made the camp trailer, providing us a place to eat and bunk. We would un-hitch the old Ford and be off wherever we could to find a place to proclaim the message of life. People would come from distant villages and ask us to come to their little town to preach.

We were invited to come to one distant village that had no roads leading to it. They said we could drive on the beach almost all the way, so off we went, ready for the adventure. Adventures for Jesus are the kind that give a lasting thrill and we never seemed lacking for them! We drove down on the beach and were getting along fine until, all at once, we hit a soft spot in the sand. All four wheels sank until the car was lying flat on its body, stuck and unmovable. How would we ever get out of that? The tide was coming in! You might say we had "had it." There was no way out; it looked like we were sunk. On the beach there were hundreds of people: some fishing and some just wandering around. It happened that one group had a great, long, heavy rope, and though there was no horsepower, there was plenty of manpower. I persuaded them to let me tie one end of that rope to the front bumper of the old sunken vehicle and then, by the use of that beautiful language, I asked them all to take hold and pull. What do you think happened? Something had to give. All I had to do was steer and soon the old "tub" was out and up on solid ground.

We showed our deep appreciation, while I was untying the rope and getting ready to go on, Mary passed out tracts, telling them all about Jesus. Here again our dear Lord stopped us to deliver His wonderful Gospel. For the rest of the way we stayed farther from the water on solid ground and soon arrived at a place called Mui Ne, another fishy smelling town. Mui Ne Beach is a district of Phan Thiet, Viet Nam, with red sand dunes and a variety of beaches. We spent several days there and many were saved. We know their salvation was real for the next Sunday at Phan Thiet where the new church had been built, we found them. They had walked the twenty miles just to meet with the other Christians and worship the Lord.

One day while still in this town, we saw a beautiful, dark skinned girl who proved to be of another race of people. She was from a section of the country occupied by the Cham people, the original people of Viet Nam. They had covered the entire country until the Vietnamese came down and drove them south. Through the years they had dwindled to about 20,000 and were confined to a small territory near a town called Phan Ri. We inquired of the girl about the people and promised we would be by to visit them.

Time flew and it really was several weeks before we got around to visit their village. When we did, we were amazed to see one of the most gruesome ceremonies one could ever imagine. A man had died in the village and they were preparing for a cremation. We camped nearby and watched the horrible sight from beginning to end. The whole procedure was turned over to a company of priests completely controlled by Satan himself. They were so drunk they could hardly walk, filled with "spirits," the same stuff that is ruining so many other people in this world. In an open field, in the hot tropical sun, they ordered the villagers to prepare a huge pile of brush on which the body was to be burned. Blankets and other clothing belonging to the dead man were laid on the brush. While waiting for the body, the crowd gathered as the drunken, staggering priests were trying almost helplessly to carry the remains to be placed on that pile of clothes, blankets, and brush awaiting the torch.

Satan surely likes to make fools of men all over the world. Where there has never been any Gospel throughout the centuries, he has done a horribly effective job. What a disgrace! They finally succeeded in getting the body up on the place where it was to be burned. But the endless ritual and ceremonies of a man-made religion directed by the devil were absolutely astonishing. On the dead body was placed candy, cake, sweets and eats of all kinds. The body had already been kept for ten days in a shed surrounded by drunken priests, who no doubt had already lost their sense of smell. By the time the body was on the funeral pyre, those who were watching chose to stand on the windward side.

Round and round the priests went with their incense, "holy" water, little leaves and bones and sticks, bewildering the crowd with their secret incantation. When they were through, they came with the fire. The dry brush was soon blazing briskly and before it got too hot, the children along with others began to grab food from the body that had been covered with the dead man's clothes. What hubbub and what a mess, while the loved ones were crying. Then came the crucial moment when the head must be severed from the body. The priests couldn't do it. They were too drunk! One of the relatives with a long bladed axe began chopping away till finally the head dropped to the ground. The priests then were called on to perform the final ceremony of cutting the forehead from the skull. These bones were put in a small basket and given to the relatives to be hung up in the roof of their little thatched house. What a reminder of such a hideous day!

We camped near the river in an open field where they usually bury their dead. You see, when they have no money and can't afford a cremation, they have to bury the body and wait for the day when they can dig up the remains or the bones for cremation. All was quiet that night but people came out the next morning looking so strangely at us. They didn't think we would ever survive through the night. They thought that open field was so infested with devils that no one could live there through the night. No doubt the devils and demons were there, but the One who said, "Go into all the world," also said, "I am with you," every day and night, too.

This poor race of Cham people had lived like that through the centuries and we were the first to ever tell them about Jesus. One of the best sermons we ever gave was on that first night. There was sweet peace and silence in the presence of the One who has all power in heaven and on earth.

This was a group of people, not Vietnamese, who had owned the whole country in years past but had been beaten down and finally concentrated in that one section of the country. The Cham people think highly of their past history when they were in full control of all that territory now known as Viet Nam. But complete surrender to Satan and all those demons had meant their destruction and near extinction. They were in unbelievably degraded debauchery, completely under the control of Satan. They didn't even have ancestor worship because they were far below that. They were down so deep that they didn't worship anyone, only Satan himself, completely given over to the devil. Now when you go into a place like that and get any results, you are reminded that it is "not by might, nor by power, but by my Spirit, saith the LORD of hosts." (Zechariah 4:6) That's the only way and we knew that.

In one of our visits to this village, we arrived in the evening only to witness one of the darkest satanic orgies. As we parked and thought of taking a little rest after the hot, tiresome day, we heard in the distance the sound of drums and gongs in the village. When drums in the dark are heard, Satan is working. We knew it did not mean anything good.

Satan was in complete control of that village; this was to be a big night for him. We made our way toward the drums in the dark. It was several hundred yards over in the midst of the village. Then we made our way down the pathways of the little village. As we arrived we saw strange things going on. They had made a long shed of bamboo with a roof of long, dry grass and a place arranged for people to sit against each wall. At the far end was a large chair arranged like a throne where Satan was invited to sit. The drums and gongs provided the uproar as they pleaded for hours for him to come and occupy the throne. A woman was sick unto death in a little hut nearby. The whole occasion was planned to call Satan, the evil one, to take his throne there and then bring her out to bow and worship as a last act.

We stood at the open entrance and watched and prayed, recognizing that we were invading Satan's territory. They would have liked us to sit down with them and take part in welcoming that awful fiend to their village and their hearts. When we came upon events like that, we would never interrupt. We let them continue and the next day did our preaching. So now we stood and waited and watched. We stayed outside and prayed. On and on they went.

Finally an elderly lady all dressed in red came on the scene and began her devil dance before the throne. What strange contortions in a devil dance! This she carried on for perhaps an hour or so. We found out that the reason for all this was that the family of the sick woman was looking to Satan for help. They took us over to the little shed to the side of the poor dying woman. What a pitiable sight, she was lying on a grass mat on the ground, in fear and suffering. We explained the gospel, telling her all about Jesus and His love, and she was really interested. When we asked her if she would right then accept Jesus as her personal Saviour, she looked at us with such wistful eyes and we knew down in her heart she wanted to say yes. But one glance at her relatives standing on her other side made her hesitate. First, she would look at us, then at them as we prayed for the Holy Spirit to overcome the power of darkness. We felt that in her heart she was ready to accept Jesus, but there was such pressure from devils and demons and the crowd around all given over to devil worship. In the midst of that came the cry, "He has come." Then we witnessed a most pitiable sight. The people literally dragged that poor old creature into the throne room while they lined up on each side, watching as they forced the poor dying woman to prostrate herself before that throne where Satan was supposed to have seated himself.

What a heart breaking scene to see that poor, helpless woman, against her will, forced to prostrate herself before the one who had brought such misery, fear, and death on her and on people everywhere. She was dragged back into that little hut to die. We stood there and cried, vowing to stay there in the days to come, proclaiming the good news of Jesus that those people might be freed from such awful bondage.

We decided to stay with them till the seed was planted that would finally produce a church in their midst. We'd go there for at least a month every year with the trailer and live right among them. It would take a book to tell their history. Our main object was to find out how we could reach through their mess of religious bondage and bring them to the Lord.

They had had a king. His tomb was still there carefully guarded. His descendents guarded some gold relics, which caused constant turmoil as different pieces would, from time to time, be stolen. That did not interest us. We were there for trophies far more precious than gold, which God was going to give. Praise Him!

The first one to accept the Lord was a member of the royal Cham family, a young man named Thiet, about 16 years old. He was young, but he knew what he was doing. He had had enough of Satan and the bondage and was so delighted to be free. His older sister was keeper of the king's gold that had been left in their midst over the years. Once in a while she would bring it out for display and when she would find some of it gone, she'd go into a frenzy and rave on for hours, pacing up and down in front of the table covered with those precious keepsakes. The whole town would gather to watch the spectacle.

We always attended these occasions with one purpose, that was to tell them of the riches far more precious than gold. After the wild, occultic orgy was over, we still had our audience set up for more of the Good News. The young descendent, Thiet, of the ancient king, was such an example of God's grace that they stood there in awe and wonder. All his relatives tried to get him to recant, but to no avail. He had changed so drastically.

He stood true in spite of all the persecution. Some of the men of the family took him down to the river and put him under. After holding him there a few moments, they brought him up and said, "Now change your mind or we will hold you under until you are gone." He staunchly refused. Not daring to kill the prince, they brought him up and finally had to let him go as he continued to praise the Lord. What a shining light in a place Satan had covered with such dark night!

Thiet grew in grace and was so anxious to know more about the Lord and His Word that he decided to go to the Bible school at Tourane, now known as Da Nang. He came from a different race and we wondered how he would get along. He was such a shining example before all the Vietnamese students that it wasn't long before they looked to him as a leader in their midst. There soon was such a marked interest in reaching the Cham people that a young Vietnamese man in the Bible school decided to go and live in their midst and be their pastor. They soon had their own thatch meeting house with their pastor and Thiet, a faithful helper in evangelizing his people.

14

Faith Works by Love!

One of our first lessons, which we learned in about 1937, was faith works by love. There is no other channel through which it can work. (Galatians 5:6) Sometimes one goes to the mission field and thinks he's quite young and cocky, and he knows just about everything there is to know. He thinks he's learned it all. He goes out there and finds that the Lord has a lot to teach him. One of those first lessons we learned was, without love, no one can be reached. You can teach and introduce the Gospel to people in their heads, but it never reaches their hearts. We had established a church in a place called Phan Rang, and sometimes when we were down there on another trip, we'd go and stay for a week or so.

On one of those trips in the southern part of that vast territory, Jesus had to bring a lesson most forcibly to our hearts. We were in the camper near the church that had been planted in the town of Phan Thiet. Early one morning, a little girl we had met in the church and

who had become a Christian asked us to please come
to her village and visit her parents. The place was about
eight miles away from Phan Thiet so we promised to
be there that day. When we arrived, she took us down
little alleys in the midst of hundreds of little thatched-
roof houses and finally into one where her parents lived.
The crowds saw us coming and they soon were gathered
by the hundreds around that little hut. We were polite-
ly invited in and seated with the wife and children. We
didn't see the man of the house, so we began talking
to the mother. We explained all about the wonderful
news of Jesus and His glorious salvation, and the crowds
listened, but they were not too impressed. Finally the
lady said, "Talk to him," as she pointed to what was
left of her husband. There he stood the most emaciated
specimen of skin and bones standing there gazing into
space, one foot in the grave…"Gan dat xa troi," they
say, "near the earth and far from heaven." How could
we ever get the Gospel across to such a creature? We
knew we had to try.

The women and the crowd were in essence saying,
"Try your religion on him." How good it is that we
had more than religion at the end of that trail! But oh,
the lesson we had to learn that day! We talked and explained all about the Lord's coming to earth to save sinners, but we could see plainly that we were not getting
anywhere and the crowd knew it, too. I saw it was just

going in one ear and out the other, perhaps not even going in. He was an opium smoker and was no doubt dreaming of his next smoke. He had been a slave to that habit for twenty-seven years, and it looked as though there was no hope. He had spent all he ever owned, home and land, just to satisfy that terrible craving for opium. The family members were just waiting for him to die and get rid of him and the expense. After trying so hard to blaze a trail deep into darkness and slavery, we saw we had made no progress at all, so I said to him, "Come on, let's get on our knees." He could at least do that. We knelt by an old rickety bamboo bed and began to pray. The crowd was pressing in from every side, having a good time watching the show. They knew that no religion or anything else could save that poor man. We were on the spot, Mary on one side and I on the other, praying.

As we prayed for the poor fellow, the Lord began to speak to us personally that something was lacking. The Lord had something to teach us and it was the most beautiful lesson, something never learned in Bible school or anywhere else. We began to talk and pray and listen to what God was saying to us. We were praying in a sort of religious, condescending way that God would do something for him. The Lord was telling us that He had to do something for us because we lacked one thing. We had studied and read about it a lot, but here Jesus was telling us in no uncertain terms, "Your faith does not work, there is only one channel through which it can work. . .and that is LOVE." From that moment on we realized that we lacked that one thing, love. We didn't love that guy like the Lord did. He wanted a channel through which His love could work.

An overwhelming revelation came over us in that unlikely place. We questioned ourselves: Did we really love that poor man? We realized that we didn't love that drug addict and the Lord had to do something for us first before anything could happen.

Our realizing that there was not love in our hearts for this wretched man truly broke us. We began to cry and pray for ourselves. That day we learned something that we never learned in Bible school. If we were going to reach people, it had to be the Holy Spirit working, giving us faith and then filling us with love and compassion for people who are so bound by sin, misery, and hopelessness.

With our hearts now broken, the crowd soon sensed the fact that we were actually not just saying prayers, but were talking to the God of the Universe. It was in their language and they were amazed to hear us actually talking to the living God, crying for help personally. Silence came over the whole crowd; the same ones who had been standing, snickering, and making fun. Now they listened quietly. God was making His presence so real that they stood at attention, pulling off the old rag or hat they had on their head, bowing their heads. After praying and calling on the Lord for our own needs, we slipped over close to the poor opium smoker, put our arms around him and began to pray for the hopeless man. That poor specimen of humanity just stood there and no one in the world loved him. Jesus did, but there had to be a channel and He wanted to use us as that channel.

The Spirit of God had found a channel through which to work; and work He did! The poor lost soul began to pray. His mind seemed to clear up and he was talking to Jesus. What a friend he had found when the glorious light of the Gospel broke through that jungle of sin and misery. He was born anew by the love and power of the Holy Spirit. After we got up from our knees we saw that his face had changed. It had a shine that had never been there before. As I looked into his eyes in real love I said, "If you really want to get rid of this terrible habit, you must leave this place and go down to the church eight miles away and stay there in the church with the Vietnamese pastor until you have no more desire for opium."

We didn't know how it would work out; we had to be on our way to another section of the country and were gone two or three months before we got back to see what had happened. Something wasn't just "about to happen," it had come to pass! What a miracle of

God's grace! One of the first persons we met on arriving back there was this precious man, completely delivered from his opium habit. He had gained so much weight we hardly knew him. He was rejoicing in the Lord. He became one of the deacons in the church, a faithful servant of the Lord, a living testimony throughout that province. Such evidence of the love and presence of the living God! People were saved for miles around. When his whole family was saved, the entire village realized something had happened and that God from heaven had visited those people. The news of that man's deliverance spread far and wide. Faith works by love!

That church grew and became prosperous in that town called Phan Rang in the south part of central Viet Nam. Finally after thousands of years the Gospel had arrived in this region too. God had come in! It was because He could teach us little helpless ones to love people - not by natural love, but the love we received from Him working through us. By love, people are brought to know Him. That's what counts.

Fellowship in His Suffering

Jesus, my dear Lord and Saviour,
As I draw up near to you,
The picture comes in focus
And I get a clearer view.

Then I see things as You see them
And my heart begins to break,
In that fellowship of suffering
By Thy grace I undertake.

What is the picture that I see?
As it stands in bold relief,
'Tis a sick and sorrowing world
And One acquainted with such grief.

Yes, He's the Man of sorrows
And the picture is so clear,
That every soul on this old earth
To the Lord is very dear.

He's not willing any perish,
But accept Him and His love,
And to be with Him forever
In that glorious home above.

So, the vision of my Saviour
And a world undone and lost,
Stirs my burdened heart to reach them
Even though at awful cost.

15

Unrighteous Mammon

(1938)

One day while sitting under a huge shade tree near the river beside our Model A and trailer, the young preacher turned to Luke, chapter 16 and verse nine. We read it together there in that strange place way off from civilization, under an old tree usually inhabited by vultures. God spoke with a strange new light on that one verse which is usually passed over without explanation. There had to be an explanation that day so we began to read. Jesus had spoken the parable and now came the application. As you know, parables and expositions without application are of little value. Jesus said: "I say unto you; make to yourselves friends with the mammon of unrighteousness...that when ye fail... no, when it fails is what it really says...they may receive you into everlasting habitations."

The light burst in upon us, right there in one of the darkest spots on earth. The Lord spoke in a new way not only to that young preacher, but to us also. Make to yourselves friends—how are you going to do that? Use every means possible, holy covetousness! A new Ford and a trailer and any equipment necessary, get it and be out with it in the blistering heat and torrents of rain, wear it out over the rough roads. These are the things that the Lord gives us to use. We're supposed to use them up. Don't try to save them, use them! Use this unrighteous mammon. Get a hold of anything you can get a hold of and use it so that when it fails, not when I fail, and it's all worn out and gone to pieces, get another one and keep on. It takes money and materials, but just spend it, wear it out, get more and use it up in order to do what? When it all fails, make to yourselves friends with it! After all, that's all it's good for.

When it fails, you'll have a treasure that's beyond anything else. Those friends made all over Viet Nam, so many thousands gone on before, where are they? They'll be waiting to welcome you as you go to those tents that will never perish, into everlasting habitations. That's worth spending everything you can get a hold of. The money or anything you can get a hold of, let it go, no matter what, so that you might win friends. Win friends so that you can bring them to the Lord. Here goes, grab everything usable, use it, wear it out, and get more!

In the 50 years serving in Viet Nam, we polished off a half dozen or more cars and two trailers. What else was it good for? Still there was so much more as the years came and went and new inventions arrived. The Lord has always been eager to get us to use up anything we could find to spread the Good News faster into the dark corners of Viet Nam. As the "Macedonian call" was coming from so many other parts, we pulled up stakes leaving the young preacher with a clear, new vision of how to make friends with "that unrighteous mammon." How good it was to have a faithful servant ready to stay there, spend and be spent, laying up treasures that never perish.

Mary loved to share the following story of what the Word of God in written form will do in the hearts of heathen souls "in the regions beyond." "There was a thickly populated section up near the foothills of the mountains in Central Viet Nam where no messenger of the Cross had ever been. We arrived early one afternoon and spent the remainder of the day witnessing and distributing tracts in the village of Ban Thach. Around sunset we parked our car and trailer loaded down with Gospel literature just outside the village. It was a beautiful moonlight night, but oh what heathen darkness surrounded us! The gongs and cymbals in the nearby temples reminded us of the powers of darkness at work.

"The shades of night fell, and we began our open air meeting. The beautiful tropical moonlight shone down upon the hundreds, yes literally thousands who came together from every direction. We would divide the crowds, Mr. Travis taking a large group, the native worker who accompanied us another, and I was speaking to a large group of women and children. I was teaching them John 3:16, 'For God so loved the world that he gave his only begotten Son, that whosoever believeth in him should not perish, but have everlasting life.' One by one they stood up and recited it from memory. To each one who memorized this verse I gave a little booklet containing many Scripture portions. The Work of God was being planted in the hearts of those pagan souls.

"Suddenly a middle aged man stepped into our midst. He was drunk, ragged and emaciated, a pitiable sight. He began shouting and making such a disturbance that it was impossible for us to continue teaching the Word. I lifted my heart to God asking for wisdom. I stepped forward with some tracts and Scripture portions and said to this poor drunken heathen: 'Here are some little booklets I want to give you. You are not able to understand what they mean tonight but I want to tell you that there is a God who loves you. In those little books you will learn more about Him. Please take them home with you and tomorrow morning when you are feeling better, learn this short verse which I have underlined with red pencil, John 3:16.' He was too drunk to realize what it was all about but he took the literature and staggered out of the circle and we went on teaching the Word.

"Fourteen months later we were spending time at Tuy Hoa in the northern part of our district about fifteen miles from Ban Thach. After the morning service I was greeting the Christians. A nicely dressed middle aged man was one of the first to greet me. He bowed respectfully according to the oriental custom, "Chao ba" and said: 'Don't you know me?' I looked at him and as he repeated, 'Don't you know me?' I said, 'I'm sorry, but I have been away so long, I'm afraid I've forgotten.' He continued, 'Don't you remember the old drunk at Ban Thach who disturbed your meeting? I'm the man, but praise God, I am not that old man now. I am a new man in Christ Jesus. God who loves me used that little book and His Word in that little booklet you gave me, that night long ago to save my poor soul. I took it home not being able to understand it that night, I remembered what you told me to do. The next morning I found the verse you underlined and I got down on my knees realizing myself a poor lost sinner, I accepted Jesus as my personal Savior. Peace came into my heart, joy filled my soul, and my life was transformed. By God's wonderful grace I have been able to lead my wife and children all to the Lord, also many others in my village have accepted the Jesus way. Today in my village there are over fifty Christians waiting for you to send us a preacher to tell us more about this wonderful Saviour who loved us enough to give His life for us.'"

Mary would conclude her story, "Yes, the printed page is one of God's most potent ways to reach the heathen in the 'regions beyond.' And only time will tell when up in glory we shall meet the countless throngs and hear them tell the story of His redeeming love, what God hath wrought through these printed messengers of the cross." It was stories like these that we commonly shared during our tours in the US telling the churches there, all that the Lord was doing in that far away land.

My dear Mary Hall Travis would later write this poem on May 12, 1971:

Love for the Lost

Can we say we love the lost ones,
Jesus gave His life to save?
Do we show it by our actions,
E'er they reach the dark cold grave?

We must tell the blessed story
Of His death on Calvary.
Oh, the death of love eternal,
Jesus died to set men free.

They are dying all around us,
Those for whom our Saviour died.
Have we stopped to hear their story,
Point them to the crucified?

They are passing, thousands daily
May God's children faithful be;
Haste the glorious message to them;
Bring the lost to Calvary.

What rejoicing up in heaven!
When we meet our Saviour there,
And the ones we've led to Jesus
Shall with us His glory share.

Onward, onward with the message,
Found in God's most Holy Word,
"Jesus came to save lost sinners,
Bought them with His precious blood."

We will praise Him, and adore Him,
Christ our Saviour, Lord, and King;
Some glad day He's coming for us;
With His ransomed then we'll sing.

Ha-le-lu-jah, Ha-le-lu-jah,
What a meeting that will be,
Ever with Him, shouting Glory
Throughout all eternity.

16

The Great Adventure

Where next? We wanted to go home for Christmas, but we could not pass through the next town and leave it without them ever hearing about the One who came that Christmas night. We knew the rainy season was soon to come to that section. But we thought we could get a good start, prepare the ground, and plant the seed. Again we found an empty room, a store front, so we rented it and set up shop. It had a boarded-up loft where we could lodge, eat, and sleep. Downstairs we placed some chairs and a big box as a pulpit. We were immediately in business. It's good we had that upper room for we were there a week or two before it began to rain. In Viet Nam, when it rains it pours. Crowds had come and listened night after night, many accepting Jesus, but it soon became certain that the floods would soon be on us and we would need that upper room. Sleigh bells and snow we never knew in Viet Nam; all the snow was liquid and runny. It came right into the chapel—not just showers of blessings, but floods of water neck deep, right in our new chapel. We were so thankful for the upper room where we celebrated Christmas that year. Of course the Model A and trailer were outside getting their bath. You couldn't hurt that Ford. That's what it was made for, to use up for the Lord. It was so completely submerged that water filled the crank case and all other parts; it sat there while we rode out the storm. Christmas is JESUS, not places and things, and with His presence He makes up for all that might be lacking. Praise Him!

We had a good Christmas rejoicing in the Lord and praising Him for the privilege of being right there with the message that gives Christmas its glorious meaning. That was a good place to start the New Year too. That was God's appointed place for us. The water did not recede until after New Year's, but it finally went back to the river and we were left to view the mess. We finally were able to clear out the mud and debris. Next was to get the wheels to turn.

As you know, sin and righteousness won't mix. Likewise, oil and water do not mix. We made use of the fact and proceeded to open the drain plug on the car and let the water run out until the oil appeared, then quickly closed it with the oil retained. After clearing the electric system, to our surprise, it began to purr as if nothing had happened. We stayed on there for several weeks and were ready for a national preacher to come and take over while we moved on to other sections of that great harvest field.

One evening, a short time before we left, a strange man from among the Cham people who lived in that part of the country came in to find out what was going on. He was an intelligent man and wanted to know in detail about the things we were telling the people. The truth rang so true to his mind and heart that he was ready to accept the Lord then and there. What a joy to see his face light up as he exclaimed, "That is just what I thought ought to be! I knew there was a good God there and He has come to save me from the power of Satan." Praise the Lord! We gave him a Bible and he was so delighted that he started to read the Word right away!

It would take another book to tell the long story of his life and heart longing for deliverance from Satan's power and to be out in the sunshine of God's infinite love. Glory to the One who finally led us to him with the Words of Life!

Much is said these days about pioneering. It is often associated with scaling mountains, shooting rapids, and blazing trails. Of course, that gives lots of adventure. For a Christian, there is something far better and beyond trail blazing. If you have to shoot rapids and blaze trails to reach people, that's wonderful, but when you get there the greatest of all trail blazing takes place. It is to reach people deep in the jungle of horrible superstition and ignorance and hidden away in the darkest night. How to reach into their darkened hearts is the most difficult undertaking of all. It can't be done apart from the special guidance and wonderful love of God. He wants to show His love through us.

Adventures

Many people seek adventure
Thrills and spills throughout the day,
But they have no lasting purpose
As their short life slips away.

Just commit your life to Jesus
Then the real thrills will begin,
As you join His rescue party
Reaching lost and dying men.

This adventure is so thrilling
So rewarding is God's plan,
Things accomplished will be lasting
And will all the ages span.

The living trophies that you gain
Will be people, living souls,
Treasures with you there in glory
As God's wondrous plan unfolds.

So we set out to blaze the trail deep into the hearts of hopeless, helpless, miserable human beings who were trapped far from God in a web of darkness. This is the most thrilling adventure that can come to a servant of the Lord Jesus Christ. He said, "Go ye into all the world and preach the Gospel," with the promise, "I am with you all thy days," making this the most wonderful experience that can come to anyone of this earth. (Matthew 28:20)

We arrive on site. That is important, but that is where the real conflict begins. Satan will then put up the fiercest fight to hold his slave in bondage. We must depend on the whole armor of God as "we wrestle not against flesh and blood." (Ephesians 6:12) The powers of darkness are too great for anyone to presume to contend with. There must be simple faith, but that faith must operate as the Lord has made clear in Galatians 5:6. As we meet those folks in their humble thatched houses, all the effort it takes to get there will all be wasted if we don't have what it takes—God's love shed abroad in our hearts by the Holy Spirit! True empathy and compassion come from above.

17

Three Years of Internment

To go into Satan's territory and reveal the evil secrets he has used to deceive whole nations is a fearful thing. The secret of survival is being with such a group of faithful people who have joined a society, The Christian and Missionary Alliance, to cover us with prayer so that through the years the evil one could not touch us. What a fellowship in such a band of prayer warriors. There is no other way to explain how we weak and helpless ones could go in spite of Satanic power to rescue men and women "alive" from the snare of those evil spirits.

The Alliance

Sometimes we forget and fail to say,
What the Alliance has meant to us each day.

A wonderful means in God's dear hand,
To carry us out to a foreign land.

There to support and carry us through,
Real prayer backing in what we should do.

> *Folks set to reach, whatever it took,*
> *The regions beyond with that dear old Book.*
>
> *We've been sustained year after year,*
> *By constant prayer and many a tear.*
>
> *Kept by God's grace to finish the course,*
> *Mindful each day of that wonderful Source.*
>
> *Wonderful people with a wonderful Lord,*
> *Working for Jesus in sweet accord.*
>
> *Laying up treasures in heaven above,*
> *Bringing them in by that "Labor of Love."*

Well, time was marching on. Soon we were off to our second furlough in 1938, never realizing what lay ahead. The days and months rolled swiftly by and we were soon off again to what was still French Indo-China in 1939. The churches were prospering and going well with their national pastors but there were still great stretches of territory yet untouched with the good news of God's love. Evangelizing and church planting were still our way of life and ministry.

Miracles of God's grace continued through the years over those four provinces. The days of war had not arrived yet, but exciting things began to happen at the end of our next furlough. World War II was on and France was being overrun by Nazis.

Meanwhile we were onboard ship in Los Angeles with five children on our way back to Viet Nam. We were surprised when we heard that the ship had to go into dry dock for painting and repairs. All passengers had to vacate the ship and be taken to hotels while they completed the work on the ocean liner. Instead of hardship which we were accustomed to, it proved to be a luxury. The ship authorities were so apologetic about our inconvenience that they taxied us to one of the fancy hotels in San Francisco, gave us meal tickets and saw to it that we lived in luxury all the time that ship was in dry dock. In the midst of it all, news came that England had declared war on Germany and as the war was rapidly spreading, they took our passports and it looked as if we would not get back to French Indo-China. However, in a few days the passports were renewed and we were on our way, praising the Lord! The way things were going in the world, one might be glad to stay home and away from all the mess, but our hearts were in Viet Nam and we wanted to be back in our adopted home. It was for life, you see.

After many bleak and stormy days, we finally arrived at Shanghai, China. As we walked out on deck, there we saw a French ship making its final trip to France by way of Viet Nam. We realized that this would no doubt be the last ship to get back to Viet Nam, but they were leaving. How could we ever within an hour get transferred with all our baggage to that ship? Our baggage was down in the bottom of the ship—lots of equipment, motors, generators and other gadgets with which to preach the Gospel. Mr. Bechtel, an Alliance missionary living in Hong Kong, was there to meet us. We told him the situation. That was our last chance for a ride to Viet Nam. Could he get enough help there on the dock to get all our stuff over on that French ship before it sailed? Since we were docked on the Kowloon side of the bay, I had to go over to the other side, which was Hong Kong proper, to get clearance for passage to Viet Nam. All this had to be done within an hour. How could all this ever be done?

My wife and children boarded the other ship and waited, watching those guys under the direction of Mr. Bechtel transfer all our baggage to the other ship. I was still across the bay, feverishly trying to hurry those papers through and get back before that ship sailed and I was left behind. The Lord knows how to take care of details, and every step of the man who is made righteous is ordered of the Lord. The old steamer was blowing its final whistle when I hit the gang plank. As it was being pulled away, I leaped through the door into the arms of my precious family. What split-second timing! The ship was completely blacked out for fear of German submarines. Thus began our first taste of war, which was to last for so many years.

We lost no time in getting back to our stomping ground in the southern part of central Viet Nam, little realizing what was near at hand in that far off land. The warlords of Japan were dreaming of what they called their "co-prosperity sphere" and were set on taking over all the Far East as their domain.

The old Model A Ford had waited a year for us to come back. First the old crate wouldn't go; I could not even turn it over. The pistons were stuck and when I took the head off I found the water had leaked into the cylinders and rusted them tight. I took a round block of wood and pounded away till I could turn it over. Then after I checked the ignition and everything, to my surprise, it decided to start! What a machine! Well, I had parts ready to overhaul it, but decided to get back up country before undertaking that job. The old tub seemed to enjoy the way back home. They don't make 'em like that now.

We carried on as usual, but noticed how many of the French officials were welcoming the Japanese in their great plans of occupying all the Far East. Different French officials told me that they might as well go along with them for it was certain that the Japanese would soon be ruling all that part of the world. Nevertheless, we stayed out of politics and went on with one thing only, preaching the word of Jesus everywhere.

We could follow the news with our little short-wave radio and were more aware of what was going on than the ones who were being fooled in Washington. Japan had their representative in Washington talking peace, but the activity we saw throughout Viet Nam showed plainly they were on their way to complete domination of all the Far East. Viet Nam served as a secret corridor for getting all their war machines into position for takeover. There was a railroad that ran the full length of Viet Nam which America knew nothing about. We saw the railroad trains coming south loaded with war materials, and saw the battleships in the bay near where we lived in Nha Trang. They already had full control of Viet Nam and they were carefully watching us, as Americans.

Then on that fateful day in the summer of 1941, as we sat eating breakfast in our peaceful seaside home in Nha Trang, the stunning news broke in upon us by way of that little short wave radio. That was it; we were prisoners of the Japanese military. They immediately told us to stay put until further orders. We were to go to Dalat, the hill station, there we would be under house arrest. We were at Dalat for quite a while. I suspected that the war was coming, but we had very little news in and out of Dalat. Then after Pearl Harbor, December 7, 1941, everything began to go bad for the Japanese along the coast of Viet Nam. American submarines were sinking so many ships that they decided to take us all down to the delta to an old French army barracks at a military camp in the town of My Tho. My Tho is located on the northern banks of the Mekong River, the largest River in South East Asia, and is the closest town in the Delta area, about fifty miles to the south of Saigon.

I loaded the old camp trailer, preparing to take what I could with us, but they would not let me drive the car and trailer down the coast road because the road passed near the great Cam Ranh Bay where they had all their fleet of battle ships stationed ready for attack anywhere in the Far East. I solved that by getting a Vietnamese fellow I knew to drive the car and trailer past that bay to a town where the road branched off toward the hill station.

We were to go by train, so we boarded the train for internment, which would last for three years. The train curtains were fastened down in the cattle type car we were in so no one could see the bay where all the fleet was, but the children peeked through some cracks and saw the harbor alive with Japanese battle ships of all kind, ready for action.

There we were stuck for the remainder of our three years under Japanese control. They were too busy to bother with us, so they turned the camp over to the co-operating French officials. Yet the Japanese came in every night to check to see if we were all there. We had to feed ourselves, by shopping at a dirty little market near at hand. There we found rice and a few vegetables but mostly we ate out of the hand of God and were fed by "ravens." The nutrition was poor and there was constant paranoia for us as parents; Mary and I worried about what was going to happen to our young family. While in the camp we saw lots of families split up and separated. Many would never see each other again. This was a concern always on my mind, but the Lord saw to it that our little family of seven was able to stay altogether in the camp. Although our family was never separated or corporately beaten, we were forcefully detained, terrorized by firing squads in the yard, and drastically underfed. Mary always seemed to find books and ways to keep the children schooled during our internment; they even came out of camp a grade ahead!

One of our fellow missionaries in camp, Franklin Grobb took sick one night and was taken to the hospital. His wife remained by his side but he would not survive his illness. Camp was very difficult and the death of Mr. Grobb was a reminder of the suffering during those years. The only way we found to get a little money to live on was through a friend from Italy which was yet a neutral nation. He loaned us money with just a word of promise that we would pay him back if and when we got out. This we did when several years later we found where he was in New York City.

Mary and I were determined to be positive during our internment. We knew this was an attack from Satan. Every night in camp, I would have all the children get down on their knees and thank the Lord for all our blessings. Even as Mary seemed to be in more pain with Bell's palsy, we found a way to thank the Lord. Time in that camp was bleak. There was little news from the outside world except through our Italian friends, who had been forced to leave their thriving business in North Viet Nam.

During that time there was negotiation and exchange of Japanese and American prisoners. Back in Goa, India, the exchanges were made. The Japanese came out from America with all their gadgets and fine clothes and luxuries, while the Americans had a little wicker basket with all their belongings in it. The ones being exchanged were the Japanese citizens living in America that wanted to get back to their country.

We had not decided to go on that first trip of the *Gripsholm*, but later, because Mary had such a severe case of Bell's palsy, with terrible pain and paralyzing of her right cheek, we decided we might as well go. She had paralysis on half of her body and she couldn't smile. We were accomplishing nothing while in camp. The Japanese searched us Americans very carefully as we left the camp. Then we were bussed from the camp in My Tho to the Saigon Airport and were transferred from there to the ship. So off we went on an old French ship the *Teia Maru* with 1500 passengers that was built to carry only 500.

The French-built ship, *Aramis*, was used as an Allied merchant cruiser. It was seized by the Japanese in April 1942 at Saigon, renamed *Teia Maru*, and used for our repatriation trip. A few years later in August of 1944, the old French ship was torpedoed and sunk by a U.S. submarine in the Philippines.[1] For now it would serve as the first part in our journey back to the United States.

On two occasions our son Paul gave us lessons on practical faith. The first was on our trip from the internment camp when we had hidden away some American money. How to get the money past the Japanese without getting caught was a problem. I rolled the money up tight and put it all in a small bottle which I put in my pants' watch pocket while we were on the Japanese ship. Unbeknown to me, the pocket had a hole, and through that hole the small bottle disappeared on that ship with 1500 people.

The children were scattered all over the ship because of the poor accommodations. Paul told us how he bunked in a small room with several other guys. I told Mary and all the children that only the Lord knew where the vial of money was. We gathered and prayed together, which was always a blessed thing to do. While we were praying Paul got a strong sense that he would find the money and told us not to worry, the Lord would answer prayer. Along with the other children in their childlike faith, he expected to find that money. Paul left while we were praying, walked out onto the deck, turned right and walked slowly looking around wondering where I might have dropped the money vial. He noticed the deck was slightly rounded – high in the middle – and sloped to the left, thinking, "If Dad dropped the vial of money here, it would roll to the deck edge." He turned walking a few feet and went directly towards four to five temporary latrines built along the rail, which were set up on deck. They were constructed over a rain collection trough that ran the inside of the deck rail. He opened the first outhouse door, knelt down, looked around and saw nothing. So he reached into the excrement in the trough by the rail. The very first thing he touched in the excrement was the little vial that had the lost money. He tried to rinse it off then brought it straight to us where the family was still in prayer. Thus, it was well taken care of by the One who takes care of even the little things in answer to prayer! The entire search and find incident took about four minutes and was the fastest answer to family prayer that we could remember. We had quite a party!

The Japanese allowed some of the Americans to make fools of themselves on that trip. The Japanese were having fun just letting the Americans get drunk when some of them got into cases of liquor on the ship. The Japanese didn't care what happened or who was killed or was thrown overboard. Some of us finally organized sort of a police force to control the situation because the men were running into women's rooms and just tearing things up. That was a hectic time all the way across to Goa, India.

The exchange liner, the *Gripsholm*, carrying 1330

Japanese civilians to be exchanged for 1500 Western Hemisphere nationals, headed for the port of exchange, Mormugao, Portugese India. The Japanese exchange liner, *Teia Maru,* with 1500 Americans, Canadians, and other Western Hemisphere nationals aboard, arrived at Mormugao at the same time, and the two groups were exchanged.

On the *Gripsholm's* trip from America to Mormugao, one Japanese deportee jumped overboard so the lifeboats set out to find him. It was infernally hot and the sea was full of sharks. The passenger was not found. When the exchange was made in Goa, there was a lot of commotion among the officials of different nationalities on shore, because there was a passenger missing, and the exchange of prisoners was halted. Finally one American offered to return to captivity, and the exchange could be made. What an unselfish sacrifice![2]

We were released from the prison of that old French ship on Thanksgiving Day, 1943 when we were transferred from the misery of internment, we looked like a bunch of cattle being herded off that old ship.

We were transferred to the Swedish liner *Gripsholm* and to luxury we had not seen for years. The *Gripsholm* was chartered by the U.S. State Department during World War II as an exchange and repatriation ship under the protection of the Red Cross, hence the term "mercy ship." The ship had the gold and blue colors of Sweden painted on her side with the word "Diplomat" lettered prominently on her side. At night, she was brilliantly lighted to show her identity as a diplomatic vessel. The *Gripsholm* was also carrying American and Canadian Red Cross supplies consisting of medicines, concentrated foods, vitamins, and blood plasma, which were intended for distribution to American and Western hemisphere nationals in Japanese controlled territories. This was the second mission the *Gripsholm* had undertaken under the United States Government as an exchange ship.[3]

There was a time during this journey when I saw bedlam in the making. All of a sudden we saw the hold of that Swedish ship's galley door open and the cook standing there. The cook asked a kid if he wanted some ice cream. Word spread fast and people started to riot over getting a bite of ice cream. I quickly jumped in and organized all the children on that boat and lined them up so all could have an equal share, rather than just a few having some, which would have resulted in turmoil.

There were lots of missionaries from China and other places on that exchange ship. That was a wonderful trip for our family. Everyone was half-starved from three years of paltry food in the Japanese prison. We got on that ship and were furnished with such an abundance of food that the children stuffed themselves. I stood there and watched our five children have food that they hadn't seen for years. Our oldest son, Jonathan, who was 15 at the time, ate for four hours straight without looking up from his plate! They had all the food they wanted.

The trip from India to New York City was nearly three months. What a voyage that was! With the war on, they could not go through the Mediterranean Sea, so they took us down around South Africa, stopping at Port Elizabeth and Rio, and up by way of South America to New York City. When we landed in New York, it was mid-winter and all we had for clothing were tropical rags, not fit for winter in New York. The Red Cross solved the problem by meeting us out at sea before reaching New York, with loads of used winter clothing, heavy sweaters, coats and other needed things. We did not care whether they fit or not; the main object was to keep from freezing. From the tropics to mid-winter in New York was quite a change!

As we finally came into the harbor we could see through the mist that grand Statue of Liberty larger than life. I don't think there was a dry eye on that ship as we beheld her beauty. We landed in New Jersey City on March 15, 1944.

America the Beautiful

America the beautiful
The land where freedom reigns,
You should either "love or leave it"
For a land still in chains.

'Tis there you'll know what slavery is
Your soul won't be your own,
'Tis there you'll bow to tyrant's rule
In bondage you will groan.

You won't stand up and speak your mind
If so you'll pay the price,
'Tis then you'll long to be back home
Where freedom is so nice.

To purchase freedom for this land
The price has been so dear,
That lawless revolution is
A thing that we should fear.

So all of us who love this land
America is our home,
Again we'll tell you "love or leave"
To where you wish to roam.

Then when your disillusioned heart
Has found things hard to bare,
We'll welcome you back home again
And with you freedom share.

We stayed in New York at the C&MA headquarters, on 44th Street in Manhattan for three weeks, wondering how we were going to get out of town. Food and gas were rationed. We were given coupons for food and enough gas stamps for the trip to Indiana.

What an outfit! Starting out in mid-winter in an old car from New York with five children, we went to Indiana and then headed to Maine. The children finished out that school year in Maine. Jonathan was in eighth grade, Ike and Paul in the sixth grade and Urban in the third. In the summer we decided to move to Nyack, New York, where we stayed during the rest of our prolonged furlough.

Evangel was 23 years old now and off to school at the Missionary Training Institute in Nyack, later named Nyack College. The boys continued on in their education in grammar school, junior high, and then high school there at Nyack.

There was another pioneer missionary family to Viet Nam who were also staying in Nyack waiting for permission to return. Irving Stebbins had been one of the first missionaries working in Viet Nam and he had gotten his family out in time to avoid imprisonment. While in Nyack our families spent a lot of time together. Tom Stebbins, Irving's youngest son recounts his memories of this time in Nyack together, "I first met the Travises on the Nyack, NY hillside where their family and our family lived at the close of World War II. Since Paul and Urb were two of my best friends, I probably spent as much time in their home and at their dinner table as my own. All of the Travis family played musical instruments: Mary and Evangel played the piano, Jonathan the saxophone, Paul the trumpet, Ike and Urb violins and Chester the harmonica. Since I played the trombone, I joined them on Sundays in the local Alliance church orchestra and often was invited to play brass duets with Paul. Like their father, all the boys were very athletic. Paul and Ike were 440-yard track stars at the Nyack High School.

"We often played pool on a miniature table in the middle of the Travis living room while listening to our favorite musicians Guy Lombardo and Vaughn Monroe. 'Mom and Pop' Travis were always sterling examples of love and godliness and unselfishly put their children's interests above any concerns for themselves or their comforts. Hence, all of the children followed their parents with unusual zeal and dedication for the things of God. With coaching and encouragement from his parents, Paul became an outstanding public speaker, winning some speech contests in the county and state and after graduation from college, became an outstanding Alliance pastor."

Because of the post war instability we couldn't return to Viet Nam right away, so we stayed at Nyack for about six years. By 1949, the three older boys had all graduated from Nyack High School. We didn't know if we'd ever return to our precious friends in Viet Nam. But finally our longest stay in America ended and the way opened to go back in 1950.

18

Longing for Viet Nam

During those years of suspense we wondered if we would ever get back "home." Even after the Japanese surrendered in 1945, turmoil continued in Viet Nam, so we were still delayed. When the time came we had to decide to either return to Viet Nam or terminate our missionary career. It was a very painful experience knowing the return would split our family in every direction. We weighed the options back and forth for some time, but the pull to the people we love was too strong! Hence, we said "yes" to His call. "We must return!"

In the summer of 1950 with an old trailer hitched behind a second-hand Dodge, we took off for the west coast. The heartaches began as we left our daughter Evangel who had just gotten married in Nyack. As it turned out, Evangel's wedding was the only wedding of all our children that we would be home to attend. Then with the four boys we headed for Seattle, Washington.

Our good friend E.R. Dunbar, who had been a

professor at Nyack was going to Seattle to become the President of Simpson Bible Institute. We left the boys under the watchful care of this trusted friend. Once in Seattle, three of the boys Jonathan, Ike and Paul entered Simpson Bible Institute, later named Simpson College, in honor of Dr. A.B. Simpson, founder of The Christian and Missionary Alliance. Initially it offered only a three-year diploma program, the school was designed to promote spiritual growth and prepare students for Christian life and service. Our youngest son, Urb, went south with us to San Francisco to board our ship for Viet Nam.

Like babies when they are being weaned, we sure did cry as we were being weaned off from our precious children, knowing we would not be seeing them for years. Urb, was not yet sixteen and was permitted to return with us; and that helped.

NOW

I dreamed of a great river wide
A crowd stood on its bank,
Discussing their plans for rescue
As a ship off shore sank.

Hundreds of people were struggling
So helpless in despair,
Could it be many on the land
Were unconcerned, didn't care?

All the boats and rafts were waiting
All ready to be manned,
But so many still insisted
A program must be planned.

They must choose a good director
In order, things must be
They must have a good committee
This clearly they could see.

They argued and they organized
The talk was long and loud,
Till everything was so confused,
No purpose in that crowd.

In the midst of all the hubbub
No one could hear the cry,
Of hundreds drowning near at hand;
How could they let them die?

The hours had passed, the night was near
There was so little time,
And when they looked the horror was
All were gone, what a crime!

Just how can we who know the Lord
Stand by in such neglect,
To rescue lost and dying souls
By sin completely wrecked?

To plan and organize is good
This work it should be done,
But those we meet along the way
Today they must be won.

Tomorrow they will all be gone
Their blood upon our hands,
Let's spread the story of God's love
To all these darkened lands.

Then when the Lord comes back again
With all that mighty host,
We'll find that personal witnessing
Has always counted most.

The ship we were supposed to go on was delayed. We didn't know why until the company called us one day and said their vessel was requisitioned to carry ammunition to Viet Nam. It was to be loaded from top to bottom with all sorts of bombs, grenades, and every kind of war material imaginable. They called us saying we could cancel our booking for Viet Nam if we wished. We had a ready answer: no cancellation. The ship was docked up the bay from San Francisco at a place called Port Chicago, where all the ammunition was loaded. This town was almost blown off the map during World War II by an accident in handling explosives. We were told that a secret taxi would get us there on time. All this activity was secret because no one was supposed to know about such loading of war material and taking it to Viet Nam for the French to use in the war with the Communists in Viet Nam. The crew was paid double to go on that ship. The last hours before leaving were feverish, for it was getting toward the close of the day, and the Golden Gate Bridge was to be cleared before dark. To hit that bridge meant there would be no more bridge, ship, or anything else around. It would be at the bottom of the San Francisco Bay and we would be in glory instead of Viet Nam.

Strange to say, we had no worries for we knew Who was directing it all. And because of that the crew was glad we were on board. As we gathered on deck for a meeting, they expressed their gladness that there was someone along who knew the One who could handle any situation. This was one voyage when we went straight to Saigon, no stopping at any port. We would not have been allowed into harbor if we wanted to stop. In 17 days, we were at the mouth of the Saigon River, ready to make that long, winding trip up that old river to Saigon. That was the most dangerous part of all; the Communists were ever ready with their mines and any other instruments of war to blow up that ship. Armed soldiers boarded the ship and off we went on that serpentine, ten-hour trip up to Saigon, but they did not go all the way to Saigon, because they did not want that load of ammunition docked near the city. The ship docked several miles down the river where the ammunition could be unloaded. We were soon escorted up to Saigon and to the land we loved, the country where we wanted to be, in spite of the horrible chaos and turmoil.

We were back again ready for another term of missionary service in 1950.

19

Work in the Delta

(1950-1955)

The war between the French and the Communists was so fierce we could not get back to our old home in Nha Trang in central Viet Nam. We were down in the Delta for five and a half years at Can Tho about a hundred miles from Saigon, beyond the Mekong River. The Mekong Delta of Southern Viet Nam is Indo-China's "rice-bowl." Much of the delta is covered with waterlogged paddies – fields of rice, the most important food in Asia. The delta is at the mouth of the Mekong River and covers 26,000 square miles.[1] The French had completely destroyed the town trying to keep it away from the Communists. The place we found to live had the back end blown off. There happened to be a room in front, so we boarded up the back and got a place to put our things in the front. We used pills in the water because the wells were contaminated. We had no lights so I made a little diesel generator for us to use. It was pretty hard going to a place that was practically blown off the map, but the people were so dear to us that we learned to love the work there in the south.

Their sons and husbands had gone north and those left behind were sympathetic with the Communists. The French were fighting to hold their colony. Those five and a half years of war were terrible. The Vietnamese were determined not to have the French there anymore.

But the French were desperate. They did things that caused the Vietnamese to lose what little respect they had for them and the people became bitter against the French. All the stores had chicken wire over the windows because the Communists would go down the streets and throw grenades through the windows.

It was time for Urb to go off to school, so we took him to the mission school at Dalat. Then we were off in our old Ford, to serve Christ in the midst of the conflict being carried on between the French and the Communists of Viet Nam. There we were in the midst of the most unpredictable fighting one ever could imagine. French soldiers were everywhere trying to hold their colony, but losing men and material every day. Travel during those five years in the midst of bombs, gunfire, and road mines put us in complete dependence on the Lord in all our work. Everywhere we saw sad sights of men bleeding and dying —not just the soldiers dying, but people killed, their homes and crops destroyed. Peasants were running for their lives, huddling along the roads in despair and hopelessness.

By the end of 1953, the Viet Minh, the Communists of that era following after Ho Chi Minh, were attacking at will. Three years earlier the U.S. had begun giving aid to the anti-Communist Vietnamese Emperor Bao Dai's figurehead government. It was a matter of too little, too late. French strength and morale steadily crumbled before the advancing guerillas.[2] In the midst of the turmoil we brought the only word of courage and hope there was in such an old sin cursed world. We managed to get to many different towns, and if a church was already there, we would have meetings throughout the day and also at night. At night the crowds did not dare travel back to their homes because they would be shot on the way, so they would pile up in the church for the night. Windows would be covered to make less of a target for Communist gunfire. Again we discovered a good time in the midst of bad times, praising the Lord in songs of worship and meeting dear friends we had not seen for years. How good the Lord is to give songs in the night, and what nights those were.

We spent a couple of weeks in a place called Bac Lieu. Day and night we were going in and out in the midst of the throngs of people. Their numbers were increased by refugees fleeing their homes. The refugees' homes and fields did not exist anymore having been burned up causing them to flee for their lives. Where there was such sad turmoil and uncertainty of life was the place to be telling people of a life of certainty with the Lord Jesus. One morning as we were about to leave for another town, my wife suddenly became ill and our departure was delayed for an hour. She was over the aches and pain in a short time and we were ready to leave. We had not gone more than two miles before we saw the reason for the delay—every step ordered of the Lord. The road was blown to pieces. A bus had gone over a mine planted under the road in the night. The bus was demolished, the dead lay beside the road and soldiers had gathered with their guns attempting to handle the situation. We stopped a while, gave out tracts, talked to the people and finally picked our way through and on to the next town. It would have been better if we had gotten there first instead of those people who died on the spot. But the Lord had many more years for us to serve in Viet Nam. Such blood curdling incidents were common as we traveled in and out among the people who needed to hear the Good News we were telling everywhere.

During those five years in the Delta another job came to hand which we had never expected. Yet the Lord had it all planned. The gospel was about to be sent out in a whole new way. On our trip back from furlough, we brought a beautiful big tape recorder intending to make recordings of sermons and songs in

Vietnamese. The recording would then be sent back to Gospel Recordings in Los Angeles, California, where Joy Ritterhoff was making phonograph records in different foreign languages to be sent back to the fields for the nationals to hear the Gospel. Our plan was to have phonograph records made and send them back to Viet Nam to be distributed to distant villages where the Gospel message had never been heard. To our surprise, John Broger, head of the Far East Broadcasting Company in Manila, visited Viet Nam with an armload of blank recording tapes to be filled with the Good News in sermons and songs which were to be sent to Manila and broadcast back to Viet Nam. He arrived in our town from Saigon in search of ways to get Vietnamese programs on the air to be beamed back to that land.

By this time we had also started the first Bible correspondence course for the Christians in Viet Nam using the Gospel of Mark, which I thought was the most easily understood Gospel. I sent the lessons to the people who lived far away whom I could not visit. When a lesson was completed, it was returned, Mary would correct it and send it back to the person with the next lesson. Then to have this broadcasting project thrown into our lap was sort of overwhelming. But we were still young and able. It was the Lord's plan, so that was what we wanted to be doing. There is always joy when we let "God's thing" become ours too.

Recording songs and Gospel sermons with people who had never seen a microphone was no easy task. We would find a shed somewhere and hang up grass mats, arranging the best acoustics possible, and work for hours to get a stack of tapes to be aired to people who lived in such darkness. We went all over the country, even up north to Tourane (now Da Nang), where the Bible school was, in order to get some of the best in song and sermon. It wasn't long before we, along with the pastors and Christians of the Viet Nam church, had prepared and recorded enough for twenty phonograph records. Soon we also had reels of tapes on their way to Manila. It was in 1951 that Viet Nam heard their first Gospel broadcast of songs and sermons over the air from Manila.

Along with the tape recorders, we also brought back the P.A. system from our last furlough. I'll never forget the day I saw a cigarette company come through the land advertising their "coffin tacks" as we saw them using their P.A. system to spread the "bad news" and throwing packs of cigarettes out for children to use. When I saw that van going through the villages using a loud speaker blazing away, I was just full of covetousness right off the bat. We were determined to have one to spread the Good News. P.A. systems were a new thing then and when I was in Chicago on furlough, I met a man who helped me get one. So it was that we came back from our last furlough with a P.A. system of our own which was wonderfully used to bring thousands within hearing of the precious words of Life. With that P.A. system we could be heard for miles around when we preached.

Meanwhile the war was going on. The French were desperate as they saw their colony slipping away from them. As you may remember, Dien Bien Phu was the last straw and the site of their final defeat. The country was divided at the seventeenth parallel and the Communists went North, expecting to be back within a year-and-a-half. The partitioning made North Viet Nam off limits to all western missionaries, and in fact to any missionaries. Not so in the South.[3]

As I mentioned earlier those were awful days when the French were desperately trying to hold their colony. Our son Urb had now graduated from Dalat School and for the rest of our term was with us traveling all over south Viet Nam. He was good at mixing with the people and could speak their language fluently. Urb would go to the market and befriend a guy pedaling a cyclo, a three wheeled public vehicle which people use as an inexpensive taxi. The cyclo driver had to pedal his customers around town. Urb would convince the driver to get into his own cyclo and then he would pedal the driver all over town in a most hilarious manner. Urb, a missionary without credentials, made friends, witnessed, and was so effective everywhere we went!

Keep the Vision Clear

With no vision people perish
By the thousands every day,
Blindness on the part of Christians
Unconcerned, seldom pray.

God's not willing one should perish
Without hearing of the way,
Why should we neglect to tell them
Let us now His word obey.

Go to all the world and witness
Of His resurrection power,
He has promised He'll be with you
Every day and every hour.

Judgment day is fast approaching
When we'll stand before the King,
Treasures that will last forever
Are the souls that we may bring.

If you've lost your love for Jesus
And the souls He died to win,
Let Him now renew your vision
Of the millions lost in sin.

Then obey "that heavenly vision"
Have the joy of winning men,
Then they'll join in praising Jesus
When He comes to earth again.

Be about your Father's business
As you mingle with the throng,
Telling of His great salvation
As you daily go along.

Use your talent, time, and money
Laying treasures up above,
All that will endure forever
Are the souls you've won in love.

What a welcome that awaits you
As you land on yonder shore,
Joining those you've won to Jesus
Ones who've journeyed on before.

Then throughout the endless ages
You'll be glad for vision clear,
To have seen the eternal value
Of the things our Lord holds dear.

20

Buying Up Opportunities

In 1955 we returned to America for furlough. After a year of visits and tours among the churches we returned to Viet Nam, leaving our youngest son Urb, who had grown to be a man, dedicated to the Lord's work.

The ship was docked at San Francisco and due to leave at midnight. What a time for such a sad parting, such excruciating pain! Separation is a painful word. A family so close during the years was now separated all over the states — New York, Washington, and California. Mary and I were being weaned to go back alone to Viet Nam. Separation is an enormous trial for the missionary! Leaving the children was the most excruciating pain, the only sacrifice worth mentioning, but God made up for it and gave more grace. God's way is the only way of peace and safety. Midnight came. There they stood on the dock waving good bye as our ship took us away into the dark night. What could we do as we got the last glimpse of our dear children whom we

were leaving behind? We hurried away to our cabin, fell
on our knees and cried like little babies.

God wants us weaned from everything
To have us for Himself alone,
He paid for us redemption's price
And we, He rightfully should own.

So if we really love the Lord
We'll welcome all this weaning,
We'll enter God's eternal plan
Life will have real new meaning.

At first we may not understand
But He will make it clear and plain,
And when we feel there is no hope
It's then we'll find all loss is gain.

If we will "study to be quiet"
We then will know that He is God,
We'll understand much more each day
The meaning of the staff and rod.

Things we think so important here
Will fade and die there in the past,
Weaned and nothing more of our own
Lost in Jesus, joy that will last.

When earth and things have fled away
And the eternal ages roll,

We'll be so glad that we were weaned
And Christ Jesus became our goal.

During the long voyage the Lord was mending our hearts and preparing us for another phase of horrible war in Viet Nam. Viet Nam was divided; the French had been defeated and their armies had left. Then the war lords of the South decided they wouldn't stand for that and started another war. Anti-communist Ngo Dinh Diem took power in a corrupt election in 1955. Thousands of angry South Vietnamese armed to fight Diem's government. Diem called them "Viet Cong" (VC), meaning Vietnamese Communists. These anti-Diem forces were led by the National Liberation Front (NLF), an alliance of political groups. The NLF was headquartered in the North, while VC guerrillas fought for them in the South. If the Communists had taken over, we would not have been able to stay in the country.[1]

I had brought aluminum louvers and other materials with me from America to build another trailer. When we got to Saigon, I built the second trailer, then we were headed up country to a parish of one million people.

We had previously been serving south of Saigon in the Delta area. This time after returning from furlough in 1956, we were stationed in central Viet Nam at Qui Nhon, in the Binh Dinh province, which had been under Communism for fifteen years. When many sons and husbands went North with the Communists, the people thought the Communists would soon be back in full control of the country.

I already shared about how our son Paul had given us our first lesson on practical faith. The second occasion came when Mary and I were saved from a horrible plane accident. Paul was at Simpson College in America and we were in Viet Nam, but distance makes no difference with the Lord.

We had just finished with our missions Conference and the days at Dalat were really refreshing for body and soul. We had enjoyed our time there as we prayed and breathed the fresh, cool air on that mountain top. Conference allocated us back to Qui Nhon and God set His seal of approval on it in a very marked way. We had to return by way of Saigon. We stayed overnight there and the next day, after waiting three hours for an old DC3 plane, we were finally in the air, bound for Qui Nhon with a Chinese pilot, not knowing the danger ahead.

The weather looked bad ahead and it looked like there would be some tough going before we landed at our home base. Clouds hung low over the mountains making it impossible to fly as one should. Planes flying over the jungle covered mountains make too good a target for the VC machine guns. So the pilot decided to get out over the sea where he could fly beneath the clouds without the danger of being shot.

As we cruised along for quite some time, we could see the storm clouds gathering in the region of our destination. Qui Nhon is a hard port to land at because of cross winds from the mountains. As we approached the town from the sea, the lightning was flashing. We were hoping the pilot would land as quickly as possible facing the storm. The airstrip ran right down to the sea so it seemed reasonable to land against the storm rather than with it. However, for some reason, the pilot chose to circle over the town and come in from the other end. He hurried with a sharp circle, banking way over as he came in by the mountain, diving for a quick landing. The cross winds were tossing us all around and finally one wheel touched the runway, the left wing almost hit the ground and at the same time the plane nearly went off the runway near a big ammunition dump. It bounded into the air and did not touch again until almost all the runway was behind us. At the speed he was going there was almost no hope – we were doomed to bounce out over barbed wire entanglements and rocks and land upside down in the sea.

But the LORD WAS THERE to set His seal of approval upon our return to Qui Nhon. All along the runway there were bulldozers, tractors, houses, and machines of all kinds, but at the very end of the strip on the right side was a small vacant patch of soft sand. The plane was going at a terrific speed and out of control, except for the mighty Hand of God which miraculously slipped us off the runway into that patch of sand. The plane ploughed into it and over a distance of about fifty yards the wheels plunged deep into that wonderful shock absorber, nosed over and stood for about five seconds, tail straight up, then fell back down on its belly in the sand. Everything that was loose flew to the front end of the plane, including passengers who had neglected to fasten their seat belts. We were seated at the back end of the plane and had a perfect view of the clutter, debris, and bodies strewn all over the cabin as we hung there by our seat belts. When the tail finally flopped back down to earth the rudder wheel was broken, but no one was hurt. The pilot sat there too stunned to move or speak. In less time than it takes to tell the story, we had made this crash landing.

We unfastened our belts and picked up our hand baggage. The steward was so dazed that he had to be reminded to open the door. The fire truck rushed up amazed that all were safe, and as the people got out, no ladder was needed since the wreck was flat to the ground. As we stepped out on the sand right beside the runway, the storm was upon us. We glanced at the barbed entanglements, the rocks and the deep blue sea where we surely would have landed upside down if the Lord hadn't planned it differently. Of the 25 passengers, no one was seriously hurt. As we stepped out, all stood there amazed. All they could say was that the God we had been telling them about had saved them from a watery grave.

Later we heard many military men who had been watching the scene say that the plane was doomed and there was no hope. There was no possible way to get stopped short of the sea. That would surely be the end of the trail and our days in Viet Nam, but GOD had prepared that landing spot, and He used that old plane to stamp His seal of approval in the sandy beaches of Qui Nhon assuring us that He still had work for His servants.

Paul told his story later and as we compared notes and the time, it was at that very time he felt lead to go up and down the halls at Simpson College and get a group together to pray for there was some special need concerning his mom and dad in Viet Nam. There surely was, for that plane was hopelessly heading for the sea, and no way to be stopped. The Lord prepared a whale to taxi Jonah to shore and he prepared a huge pile of sand to keep that plane from going upside down into the sea.

The folks from the plane came up to us afterwards and shook our hands and said how glad they were that we were on that plane...and how glad we were for the group that prayed with Paul for us on the other side of the earth!

In April of 1956, Mary and I celebrated our thirty-sixth anniversary and I wrote the following poem to Mary:

Through thirty-six years
We have lived together,
With joy and some tears
And all kinds of weather.

My love has not changed
As the years come and go,
Though far we have ranged
It continues to grow.

So on we're going
In the plan of the Lord,
Our love ever growing
In happy accord.

-*C.E. Travis*

It was in 1957 young Tom Stebbins returned to Viet Nam following in his parents footsteps to minister in the land of his birth. We knew him as the son of pioneer colleagues and a close friend of our youngest boys. He would eventually be named as our field chairman but that is getting a little ahead of the story. Tom remembers his early days on the mission field, "After graduating from Nyack Missionary College, my wife Donna and I were assigned to serve in Viet Nam as Chester and Mary's missionary colleagues. Hence, we had opportunity to meet them every year at the Viet Nam Field Conference. Mary's narrative reports of their ministry in South Central Vietnam were always punctuated with big grins, flowing tears and accompanied with laughter and applause from all those present. One reported incident made an unforgettable impression on this young missionary's heart.

"Mary described graphically how their old Mercury suffered a sudden blow-out, how Chester patiently jacked up the back-end of the car and changed the tire while she quickly armed herself with literature, went up and down the highway passing out Gospel tracts and witnessing to all that would listen. Not one minute or opportunity would be wasted in their consummate zeal to bring salvation to lost men, women and children of every age and occupation! What an incredible example for this young missionary who was in language study preparing to take the same Good News to the province just south of them!

"On one happy occasion, Donna and I were privileged to visit their station at Qui Nhon and spend some time with them in their home. Their love and commitment to each other was remarkable! Someone has said that people become like what they look at and in what they become most absorbed. That was so true of Chester and Mary! For years they sat across the dinner table and admired one another so much that as time passed by, they began to look and act more and more like one another. It was uncanny to see a twitch in Chester's face and not long after see Mary twitch exactly the same way. We laughed when Chester pounced up the stairs two at a time, and when, sure enough, right behind him, Mary full of spunk and vigor ascended the stairway in like fashion!"

Qui Nhon would be our home where we would live for years and we know more people there than any place in the world. We would try to be with one of the churches in those four provinces on Sunday, then off to the distant villages with the people, telling how God loves and wants to deliver them from the bondage of Satan.

In the midst of it all the war clouds were hanging low and the Vietnamese generals in the south were preparing to resist the Communists' return south to rule the country. Little by little the soldiers from the north were infiltrating the south, determined to take over. And by God's grace we were determined to stay. Little did we realize what was ahead as we continued throughout that vast untouched territory where they had not yet heard!

The urge of the Holy Spirit was to get to all those "regions beyond" before it was too late. Many times God used the wrath of man to keep the doors open. If the Communists had succeeded in taking over immediately as they planned, we would have been out many years before. The war, though horrible, afforded us the extra years needed to proclaim the message far and wide. We were out in their midst under God's care and direction, preaching the Word and planting churches, doing everything possible to build up the national church in their faith that they might stand in the stormy days ahead. The days did get stormier as time passed. In spite of it all, the love of Jesus so constrained us that we could not think of leaving. Looking back it seems strange to say, we sort of got used to the mess. However, we could not get used to hurt men, women, and children dying everywhere. The best we could do was to get to them with the Word before it was too late.

"Buying up opportunities" is a phrase commonly used in relation to Christian work. How appropriate it was in Viet Nam. In the business world, even in everyday life, people are usually looking for bargains. These very opportunities were everywhere in Viet Nam during those years. We were returning one afternoon from a distant village when there beside the road sat a mother and her children crying as if their hearts would break. We stopped and there in their midst we could see the reason why. The husband and father had been shot dead and they were overwhelmed with grief. We found that they were far from home, with no way to get the body back there. They told us where they lived, which was several miles away and in Communist-infested territory.

We could not leave them there. We did something no Vietnamese would do. They were so surprised when we said we would take them all home, including the dead body of their loved one. We carefully put the body in the trunk of the old car and away we went over dangerous and winding roads along a wide river where there was usually much fighting. We arrived safely as the whole village came out to see such an unusual sight, an American venturing into such a place with a dead body in the car. They soon learned why we did it, as we told them of the love of Jesus and how His love so constrained us we could do nothing less. Such acts of love and mercy always prepared hearts to receive Jesus as their personal Saviour. People had grown accustomed to seeing carelessness and indifference among their own people but when they saw the loving attitude of Mary and myself, many were already won. They saw us not as American strangers but as loving and caring friends whom they could trust. Buying up opportunities…we were finding treasures in the midst of the rubble of war. Praise the Lord Jesus!

Again as night was closing in we were hurrying back to our home base when we saw ahead a three-wheel cycle car with an old hammock hung up inside and someone in it. We supposed, as usual, someone was wounded and hurrying to the hospital many miles away. They crossed a bridge ahead of us and then stopped beside the road. Our first impulse was to hurry right on, but a second thought, under the Lord's direction, we stopped to see what was the matter. We found the poor woman was about to give birth and their three-wheeler wouldn't go any farther. What would they do? We said, "Come on, put her in the back seat of our old car and we'll get her there before the baby arrives." What an opportunity to "buy!" As she lay in the back seat we stepped on it for those miles ahead and arrived at the hospital just as the baby arrived, timed just right. People gathered around amazed that any person from far off America would stop to do such a thing. Actions like that gave way for words, and praise the Lord we have the Words of Life. In those terrible war days there was no end of such opportunities and we were always in the "buying mood." Oh, the throng of people, treasures already over in glory land, because God's people in America kept us covered with a barrage of prayer that we might weave in and out among the people and "snatch them as brands from the burning." (Jude 23)

The years just kept rolling on and we were quickly celebrating our 40th Wedding Anniversary. Mary wrote the following poem on April 22, 1960, while we were home in Qui Nhon.

Forty years of richest blessing
Jesus ever near,
Lives enriched by His possessing
All we hold so dear.

Trials come, yet Jesus caring
All the shadows flee,
And the sun shines ever brighter
As His face we see.

Little jewels, sent from heaven
Make our hearts rejoice,
As we gave them back to Jesus
One sweet girl, four boys.

He has kept them, He has blessed them
Precious in His love,
We must pray and fully trust them
To His care above.

So we travel on life's pathway
Looking up to Him,
Sacrifice, yes, gladly offering
To our Lord and King.

As we pass this happy milestone
Hand in hand we go,
Leading others to His love feast
Heaven is our goal.

Blessed Jesus, we adore Thee,
Life is all worth while,
As we trust in Thee completely
And can see Thy smile.

On together, ever faithful
May we bring to Thee,
Richest treasures—souls made spotless
From the Vietnamese.

Then some day in Glory yonder
Every victory won,
Singing praises, shouting glory
To the blessed Son.

Oh, the joy of serving Jesus
He's the one we love,
We will shout His praises forever
In that home above.

-Mary Hall Travis

It was then in March of 1961 while stationed at Qui Nhon we decided it was time to write the following update letter to our dear supporters:

DEAR FRIENDS,

In the midst of the endless calls from every quarter of this province, it seems impossible to answer the stack of letters before us so we know you will understand why we have to resort to this printed letter to keep you informed as to the work here.

"Where there is no vision the people perish." Proverbs 29:18. "The Word of the Lord was precious in those days; there was no open vision." 1 Samuel 3:1. In other words, the Word of the Lord was unusual in those days; there was no public vision. The Word was not made known.

Throughout the years Binh Dinh province in Viet Nam has generally been regarded as a very unfruitful section of the country, thus the work and workers have naturally gravitated to other parts and there has been no "public vision" here...the Word has not been made known.

Time and tide, war and privation, along with the emptiness of man-made religion has brought about a great change in the attitude towards the Gospel. The common people now hear the Word gladly, that is if there is anyone to tell them. The fact that after almost half a century of work in Viet Nam this province of over a million people remains for the most part unevangelized. There are only two missionary couples, one native pastor and four student preachers for this great section of Viet Nam. It is a mission field in itself. Binh Dinh province has a population comprising at least one tenth of our present responsibility in Viet Nam. Here the people perish, there is no open vision, the Word has not been made known. How can it be when there are so few to make it known?

Our hearts are rejoicing to see such ready response to the Gospel. Many souls have accepted Christ and a goodly number have gone on with the Lord and have been baptized. Others are awaiting baptism. The country work is especially encouraging. As you know the Qui Nhon church has gone through many trials and testings the past four years. Since it is the only church which has a pastor the entire district has been affected. Please pray that God may heal all the wounds, send Spirit-filled men for leaders and that we may see a glorious revival, victory in spite of all Satan can do.

...We believe in the "Key City" projects, but the fact remains that the great mass of people live in the country. This is an agricultural country and we know by experience that the greatest and most permanent results are found at the "grass roots" of this land. Where the poor have the Gospel preached to them there is response and a permanent work is established in their hearts, their homes, and their villages. Jesus said: "The Spirit of the Lord...hath anointed

Me to preach the Gospel to the poor." James says: "Hearken my beloved brethren, hath not God chosen the poor of this world, rich in faith and heirs of the kingdom which He hath promised to them that love Him?"

Many souls are being saved everywhere we go, but it is only a drop in the bucket as compared with what should be done as we face this present emergency. Faithfulness and loyalty are found among the poor people. When someone loves them, they respond. Just recently we found time to go to a place called Cat Than, down near the sea. It is about twenty miles off the beaten track. We had met ones several times from this far off section. They had actually begged us to come and give them the Gospel. During two days there, more than twenty-five accepted the Lord, and many others were ready to do the same if we could only stay longer. Rainy season was on and we realized the danger of the roads being broken, bridges out, and we would be trapped there and unable to keep all the promises we had made to go to other places. So we left them with a promise to return as soon as possible. In spite of all threatening and persecution, they are standing true. Every Sunday morning they have good representation at the

Binh Dinh chapel. They walk twenty or more miles through mud and water to attend the regular service there.

...With such a small force we are doing all we can to hold the "beach-heads." Our only hope is an adequate coverage of prayer...a barrage that will hold back the enemy until reinforcements arrive. Please pray that God will send in real Spirit-filled men and women with a passion for the lost and a clear vision, so these poor people do not perish."

All through the years we spent in Viet Nam Mary wrote letters nearly every week to our children. The separation was so painful yet we tried our best to keep in close contact. Mary would use carbon paper and carefully put it between sheets of very thin "rice" paper to type letters on. She would start the letters with "Dear _____" then after completing the letter she'd carefully separate each of them. Then taking one letter for each of the children and typing their name in the top and always typing a personal note to each one at the bottom. All those years in Viet Nam, this is how Mary and I would keep up with our children. Many times Mary would also write a special poem to a child for his/her birthday.

On July 10, 1963, Mary wrote the following poem to Paul for his birthday:

To Paul From Mom:

It's midnight, Paul, the lights are low
I'm dreaming, dear, of you.
Your letter here upon my desk
Has set my heart aglow.

Sweet mem'ries of those happy years
When you a little boy,
Came to our home with all your love
Pride of our hearts, our joy.

And through the years how faithfully
Our God has answered prayer,
Your life He guarded from all harm
Kept by His love and care.

He led you, blessed you, called you
And in His plan divine,
He made of you His servant
This precious boy of mine!

And as we gaze upon your face
In picture on our wall,
We think, "It pays, it satisfies
To give our best, our all."

Dear Paul, God bless you, darling,
Is Mother's constant prayer,
May He who plans the future
Continue with you there.

We'll tell salvation's story
And call His "lost sheep" home,
To Him be all the glory
For every Vic'try won.

Let us be faithful as He leads
And some day by His grace,
We'll shout His Hallelujahs
When we see Him face to face.

How good the Lord had been to us. In spite of all the separations and disadvantages, all our children graduated from Bible school; two ordained preachers, Paul and Urb, and all seeking to serve the Lord in whatever way He has led them.

They say that bamboo is the king of the Vietnamese forest. Bamboo symbolizes moral integrity. There is a Vietnamese proverb that is full of meaning, "Young bamboo will bend with ease; impossible when grown to trees." How true. We had the joy of seeing our young bamboo bend with ease and yield to the Master's fingers. Not one of our precious children rebelled or hardened their hearts. Even when bamboo becomes tangled, God's wonderful spade clears out the dross to give it more room to grow and in turn they become all the more beautiful.[2]

21

Loud Speakers for the Lord

Meanwhile the old earth kept rotating and at the same time orbiting the sun, bringing our next furlough around, and the calendar was saying August 1961. We were happy that we would be seeing our children and friends in America, but reluctant to leave in the midst of such a harvest time. During our furlough year we enjoyed happy times with our children and also visited many churches to report what was happening on the other side of the earth as they continued covering that far-off field with prayer. The days of the old sin-cursed earth just kept rolling along, and we were soon back in the midst of the conflict. The conflict wasn't just men at war, but the onslaught of the powers of darkness dragging poor people down that road to misery and destruction.

It was in 1962 while we were home on furlough that a group of Viet Cong bounded from the jungle and surrounded and captured Dan Gerber of the Mennonite Central Committee, and then two C&MA Missionaries, Archie Mitchell and Dr. Ardel Vietti, near the leprosarium outside of Ban Me Thuot.[1] When we returned from furlough there was still no word as to what happened to those three missionaries.

During the latter part of 1962 the troubles of South Viet Nam escalated rapidly. Then in March of 1963 on the road from Saigon to Dalat a group of Viet Cong stopped a Land Rover carrying two families from Wycliffe Bible Translators. Both of the men, Elwood Jacobson and Gaspar Makil, were killed along with Gaspar Makil's young daughter Janie. Their wives and other children were not hurt. The murders on the Saigon-Dalat highway came less than a year after the Viet Cong abduction raid at the Ban Me Thuot leprosarium. People in the homeland began showing more concern for missionaries in Viet Nam. *"Thou wilt keep him in perfect peace, whose mind is stayed on thee: because he trusteth in Thee."* Isaiah 26:3 reminded us of that real peace that only comes from the Lord.[2]

General Ngo Dinh Diem had risen to power in the South and was putting up strong resistance to the Communists, but his time was over. In the midst of bickering and feuding among the generals in the South, he was killed. It was in late 1963, Diem was overthrown and killed, and President Kennedy was assassinated a few weeks later. Others took over one after another, and finally, as you know, America stepped into the most chaotic conflict ever known on the face of this earth.[3]

We were at our home base in Qui Nhon at the time

when huge shiploads of G.I.'s disgorged their human cargo onto landing barges and landed them on the sandy beach in our town. The war had taken on a new phase, and now American soldiers were out there in the jungle hunting Communists. They were surprised to find us two old Americans there in the midst of such strange circumstances. They soon established a hospital, a post office, a P.X. and all the facilities necessary for an up-to-date airbase. The best in Viet Nam! We thought this was very good and so interesting. They were so kind to us, and the Vietnamese especially, as they had so much surplus building material and were anxious to help us in the church planting and building all over that province of a million people. The sad thing was the price they were paying in human lives. What a mistake to try to find and destroy the enemy in the jungles of Viet Nam when they had the ways and means to do it all in a few months. But politics was not our business, we were in the business of "buying up opportunities" and saving souls.

Nevertheless we went about the main business of telling the Good News just as we had been doing all down through the past 40 years. The war escalated to the latest way and means of fighting—tanks, big guns, helicopters, rockets, and grenades—and since there was no front, things could blow up anywhere in town or country. Qui Nhon, our home base, was the main target for Communist attack.

Qui Nhon
Written on August 16, 1963

What joy divine and peace in knowing Jesus
Though cares and foes surround me all the time,
He whispers, "Do not fear, for I am with you
To love, protect and bless, dear child of mine."

Sometimes the way is dark with many shadows
The way He leads has many valleys deep,
But still He whispers, "Child, I've gone before you,
Fear not, the clouds will lift; I'm with my sheep."

So why should I be anxious, sad or lonely?
My Lord is always with me, by my side,
His loving arms enfold me, and assure me
That throughout all the days, He will abide.

Oh love divine, what joy in knowing Jesus
Who paid my debt of sin on Calvary,
He died, He lives, forever interceding
Is coming back Himself to welcome me.

So as I walk life's journey ever praising
My Saviour, Priest, and King; He's all to me,
I'll faithful be, in getting out the Story,
He died for all, His love can set men free.

So won't you come to Him your sins confessing
Receive Him in your heart, He died for you?

187

He'll save you, give you joy beyond measure,
And peace that passeth understanding, too.

Though trials come, your path leads through the valley,
He's ever near, no fear your heart will know,
With Jesus with you, burdens will grow lighter
So praise His Name, the future's all aglow.

Yes, no one satisfies that heart like Jesus
His love has won my heart, I know He's mine.
He waits to save you, too, if you'll receive Him
His joy you'll know, His peace, His love divine.

"But we desire to let you know brethren, of the grace of God which has been bestowed on the churches of (Binh Dinh province); how while passing through great trouble, their boundless joy even amid their deep poverty has overflowed to increase their generous liberality. For I can testify that to the utmost of their power, and even beyond their power, they have of their own free will given help." 2 Corinthians 8:1-3 (Weymouth)

Hair-raising incidents were common in those final years in Viet Nam, but the main stories are around the conflict of the ages. Going into the midst of it all and taking people "alive" for Jesus is most important. Come with us on one of these thrilling experiences several years earlier.

We were led to go with the old car and camp trailer over a mountain trail to a large valley where thousands of people had never been reached with the Good News. We planned on an extended open-air evangelistic campaign. We drove into the main town of the valley to let people know we were there, but they did not know what for. We went out in the open field alongside a beautiful, quiet river and set up camp. They were so curious that it was not long before the field was full of people wondering what was up.

It was getting along toward night, so we hurriedly prepared for what America would call a show. It really was a show to them. They had never seen such an outfit—the camp trailer, loud speakers and electric lights, all bought with "unrighteous mammon" and to be used "to make friends," friends that last forever, throughout all eternity. The sun went down as usual and then that beautiful moon came up to smile on the undertaking. It was not just the moon that smiled. The Lord surely smiled on us that night and the many nights to come as we continued there with something "new under the sun" for them.

We brought some of the young preachers with us to let them learn how it is done when you are fishing for men. I remember one night, the beautiful moon, was so bright we could read by its light. As the evening came on, the crowds began to gather. As we lit up for the evening and turned on the P.A. system, the area all around in that quiet valley began to fill with thousands of hungry-hearted people. They sat on the ground to hear two strange Americans and national preachers tell the most wonderful story in all the world. I never saw so many people there on the rice fields, which were dry because the rainy season had passed. They came by the thousands. I don't know how many thousands sat down there. We had batteries running the P.A. system and some lights. As they came and sat there, we started to preach to the people. My wife played the baby pump organ, sending such sweet music out over the valley and hills. All could be heard in that quiet, moonlit night and from many miles away they came running to see and hear what it was all about. We continued on and on until it was 11 or 12 o'clock and they still stayed. The thing I want to mention particularly was the wonder of the P.A. system that would reach so far out toward the mountains to people who didn't know we were there. They soon found out.

One family in particular had lived there for years. He told his story afterwards, but I'll tell it to you now. He had been saying to his wife that there must be a God in heaven. He told her that their bowing down before those altars worshipping devils and demons and Buddha and all that, wasn't right. There's a God that rules the heavens, but we never heard from Him. Then one evening when we were down below with the loud speakers on, he was sitting there in his home, so sad and disappointed with life. He had been talking to his wife about how foolish it was to carry on the way they were doing. All at once he heard in the distance, "God so loved the world," in their language of course. So he stepped to the door and listened again, hearing the beautiful music. It seemed to be coming from the sky, out there in the distance. He stood there bewildered for a while. As he heard more, he finally broke loose and started down that mountain pathway toward the noise and music. He finally made his way, stumbled into the crowd and sat down. He was so amazed at what he was hearing about the Lord, the living God, Who he knew was there, had actually come to this earth long ago. He had never heard until then. He sat there and listened until midnight, and was amazed at the story he heard.

He said to himself that's just what we know ought to be but we'd never heard before. He sat there all evening. When we stopped preaching we went down into the midst of the crowd. A group of women gathered around my wife. I had another gang, and the national preacher another.

Along about two o'clock in the morning, this man was still there, waiting patiently to learn more about what he had heard and what it was all about. There we were with him, at two in the morning, fully explaining the Gospel to him. He was just amazed. We saw the most unusual picture you could ever imagine, that man kneeling down beside our old car, there in the beautiful moonlight on his knees in prayer.

The moon had been there for all these centuries. And here, at last, this man had heard the Good News, how Jesus loved him, had come into the world and paid the price for his sin. And he, there on his knees, prayed. I stood there and just looked on. It was such a beautiful sight, not just the moon, not just the beautiful river, not the wonderful tropical foliage around, but a man talking to God for the first time with full assurance that he was saved. The working of the Holy Spirit had changed him so completely. He was just amazed.

Then he got up, the happiest man. That man stood true all down through the years. He finally had a little church up that way in his section of country. Before leaving Viet Nam the final time, we met him, going on, true to the Lord and faithful. What a wonderful privilege to be able to reach him. If we had not had this P.A. system to reach miles up there in the mountains, he might never have been any different. He might have gone through life and never been saved.

What a privilege and what a glorious thing to think we could utilize such wonderful inventions, especially as ways and means to reach the hearts of people even miles away, and in that beautiful valley there with thousands and thousands of people waiting. They heard the Good News and this man was one of many who accepted Jesus as his personal Saviour.

After many nights in that place with such happy

results, we had to go on to many other places still waiting to hear for the first time. In the meantime we were able to get the use of a new electric generator, a movie projector and a big screen, not to show "Hollywood" stuff but to portray the glorious gospel to ones who had never seen or heard. Our slogan was "to the regions beyond" and that is where we went, even with such up-to-date equipment. How good it was to have such wonderful means to attract and get the attention of thousands of people right out in the country where most of the Vietnamese people live. Our goal was to use our equipment, or wear it out! Our purpose was "to make friends." One day our equipment will be gone, but we Christians will go to those mansions in Heaven, that never perish.

That is the way it was when we pulled into another vast river valley to preach the Gospel. This place was near a river where the bridge had been blown up, half of it still hanging in the river. When we got set up for the attack, crowds were already there to see something they had never seen before — such beautiful movies of creation, "The Prior Claim," and "The Red River of Life," etc. We turned off the English narration and explained it all, in their own language, and what an impression it made on those people!

They just sat for hours drinking in the truth in God's Word which *"will not return to Him void."* (Isaiah

55:11) After showing the films and explaining them to the people, they were not ready to go home. They wanted more, and though weary and tired, we continued on into the night preaching. Of course the war was on, but we could do nothing but press the battle right into Satan's territory.

Everywhere we went the message was so new and glorious, the people just drank it in and wanted to know more. They would gather anywhere to hear more and as soon as they knew about baptism, they wanted to follow the Lord in that. Older people were so stirred about the Good News, the power of God unto salvation, the "dynamite of heaven" blasted them right out of their superstition and sin and molded them into a new life in Jesus. It was a wonderful sight to see such joy on an old wrinkled face as the joy of the Lord filled them. In that place just mentioned, a church was soon established and a preacher sent from the Bible school to take over. We stayed around for a while and helped instruct them in this new way of life. Then later they were all ready for baptism.

On one occasion the crowd was standing on the river bank. Christians were singing as my wife was playing the little pump organ. One by one they were stepping down in the water for their turn to be baptized. One dear old lady was in the water waiting. She was so happy and enthusiastic she couldn't wait, so she ducked under the water and came up saying (it's done already).

Praise the Lord! God surely loves simple-minded people. He cares for them and they grow to know Him in a most intimate way. To tell of the hundreds of interesting, exciting, and dangerous experiences that happened over the years would take a book, but, of course, that is not our purpose at this time. To reach people during such turmoil and conflict involved going. Jesus said "go" and His love constrained us to go, weaving in and out every step ordered by One who knew the way. We were sure that He Who called us into such strange pathways had everything timed just right, not ahead of schedule and not behind.

22

Lighthouses

During our last term in the province of Binh Dinh, many hundreds accepted the Lord in distant villages and were faithful in church attendance, coming long distances by foot, horse cart, or by bicycle if they were fortunate enough to have one. They were able to support the work, and so it prospered. But now a "great trial of affliction" is upon them. Christians who used to be able to get to church bringing their tithes and offerings, now find themselves without any means of support and are forced to abandon their homes and remain in their villages where they are under complete control of the Viet Cong.

On May 21, 1965 I wrote the following update to Rev. L.L. King of The Christian and Missionary Alliance Mission:

> *"Just a few words of greeting and to let you know how we are getting along at Qui Nhon. We are so thankful that we are still here and have the multiplied opportunities in the midst of many*

*horrible circumstances. The war is bringing peo-
ple into the towns that we otherwise would never see. Qui Nhon has so many refugees that they
have had to forbid any more coming in…This
place is a prize that the V.C.'s have tried hard
to take, and are still trying. Many terrible incidents are taking place all the time. It is a miracle of God's grace that we are kept with perfect
peace in our hearts in the midst of such confusion. The roaring of planes and helicopters overhead, the constant bombing, mortar fire, and the
sharp reports of other heavy artillery during the
day and often all night keep us conscious that we
are in the midst of war. At the time the hotel was
blown up, the V.C. almost succeeded in taking
the town. We were completely surrounded, big
planes that were taking the dead and wounded
Americans to Saigon were even shot at as they
flew away from the airstrip. Not a wink of sleep
that night, but the Lord sustained. Praise Him.
Since then every military man has been on his
toes many times doing double duty. One night
since then, fifteen mortar shells landed in the
midst of town, three within a block of our house.
One neighbor lady was killed, but we do not
know the number of casualties. Now they are
using flares and tracer bullets at night to locate*

the enemy. All this does not promote sleep, but the Lord's grace is sufficient...

"*Just the other day we were surprised as we listened to the Armed Forces Radio Saigon to hear them say a missionary in Viet Nam on furlough had stated that the bombing of North Viet Nam was the right thing to do. Then there was quite a lengthy comment on what one missionary had said about the V.C. We were disturbed to think that one of our missionaries on furlough should be tempted to make personal comments especially to newsmen and have it broadcast out here. As we understand missionaries are supposed to stick to their line of duty and if any comments are made they should be made by ones in official position. Such things as were said might jeopardize the mission and missionaries, especially our "captive three" out here. We know that you will agree that the Church and all missionaries should stay outside of political and military affairs and not let 'news sharks' get a chance to quote us. We are writing to you thinking that perhaps missionaries on furlough may need to be briefed again on this subject.*

"*It is kind of wearing to be in the midst of such turmoil, distress and bloodshed continually for twenty-five years. We wonder at God's grace, and do thank sincerely all the dear folks at home for their wonderful sustaining prayer help. Praise the Lord."*

Tensions of war were increasing, the communists becoming more and more bold. By night they came in to plunder and kill; in the daytime they either flee to the mountains or mingle with others in the villages. Every day we hear of new incidents of suffering and bloodshed. While visiting a country church, Christians told us of terrible things that had happened the night before: seventeen killed in one village and thirty in another. Many faces were missing from the congregation, but it was encouraging to hear the note of victory in the prayers that ascended to the throne that day.

During this period of great tension Grady Mangham, the Field Director called and said, "Travis you better pack up and go home." My reply was, "No." "Well, at least let us bring you into the larger city where it's safer," Grady pleaded. I assured him: "These boys will take care of us," meaning the American soldiers whom we had come to know and love as well as the Vietnamese. We knew our real safety was in the Lord and being right in the center of His will.

In 1968 I wrote an update on our province titled "Lighthouses."

" 'Ye are the Light of the World, a city that is set on a hill cannot be hid, neither do men light a candle and put it under a bushel, but on a candlestick and it giveth light unto all that are in the house. Let your light so shine before men that they may see your good works, and glorify your Father which is in Heaven.' Matthew 5:14-16

"LIGHT! What a mystery, yet so practical in a dark world. Darkness is so fearful. In Viet Nam the night has been so dreaded for almost 25 years – 'the terror of night.' Truly the darkness shrouds such terror. A light is so welcomed in the midst of the awful destruction. Lighthouses – beacon lights on the rocky shore, or on a treacherous mountain, have such a friendly appearance as pilots of planes or ships see them in the distance and are guided to port or terminal.

"During our 42 years in Viet Nam, so many of these years in the midst of war we have seen many marvelous things God has done in spite of all the opposition of the real enemy, Satan himself. Evangelism has been the order of the day. From Camau, the southern part of the delta to the city of Da Nang, the Word has been preached. Thousands upon thousands have seen the Light, and countless numbers have crossed over to the other side, and are waiting to 'welcome us to the habitations that never perish.' For a period of about 15 years previous to the Armistice dividing Viet Nam, Binh Dinh province was closed to the Gospel. The Viet Minh had control of this huge territory of 1,000,000 souls. We came here in 1956, and the past twelve years here in Binh Dinh Province have been most rewarding. Many thousands have been called 'out of darkness into His marvelous light.' But for years it was almost impossible to build churches. War had brought such poverty and distress that there was no money, nor means whereby a church could be built. Only little dismal street chapels were used as we could find places to rent here and there.

"Now the picture has changed since the great U.S. military build-up. We marvel at what God has done in the past three years. A province of a million people that had no church buildings now has *ten beautiful churches* dedicated to the Lord. These are wonderful instruments in God's hands which will stand as beacon lights in this dark land till Jesus returns. How could all this be done in such a poverty stricken land? God has made it possible through the love and dedication of the U.S. chaplains directing their men in sacrificial giving of money and material to erect these Lighthouses.

"What a joy it is to visit these churches throughout the province and see the happy Vietnamese congregations as they gather to worship God. How they appreciate the kindness and love of all these faithful servants of God and all the American boys out here who are not hiding their light 'under a bushel' but are contributing much by material help and prayer. The Lighthouses are there in the midst of this horrible darkness. The pastors and Christians need your prayers in these awful days. Don't forget to pray for them, the Lighthouse Keepers, that they may keep the lights all trimmed and burning bright in order that thousands of others may see the Light and be guided safely Home."

In spite of all the enemy can do to hinder, we saw the blessing of God throughout the province. Everywhere souls were being saved; in the chapels, on the street, in the bookstore, in homes, in hospitals and in the market places. God is using the wrath of man to praise Him. Our bookstore and reading room there in Qui Nhon was a real evangelistic center. It was open every day and many inquirers were finding the Lord as their Saviour.

It was wonderful to be able to witness in the hospitals also, where they were bringing in the wounded everyday with bodies maimed and suffering, but with hearts hungry for some unknown thing. What a joy it gives us to be able to point them to Jesus *"the Lamb of God, which taketh away the sin of the world."* (John 1:19)

We thank God for the many hearts He has prepared to receive the Word and be saved. We prayed as never before for the suffering, war-torn land of Viet Nam.

The words of A.B. Simpson, founder of The Christian and Missionary Alliance, ring out in his hymn, "Jesus Giveth Us the Victory."

There's a battle raging in the heavenly places,

Sin and death and sickness with Satan leading on;
With the hosts of earth and hell against us,
How in all our weakness shall the fight be won?
Jesus giveth us the victory.
He, who overcame on Calvary,
Overcomes again in you and me.
Hal-le-lu-jah! Jesus gives the victory!

"Jesus Giveth Us the Victory"
by A.B. Simpson 1843-1919
Hymns of the Christian Life, p. 354.

We were going down into the southern part of our district with our little trailer to have evangelistic meetings and we preached for a week at Phuc Tuy, in that part of the district. Every night we had a glorious time and souls were being saved, and one night there was a little girl about 12 years old that came to the altar who got gloriously saved. Oh, she was bubbling over with joy as she rose from her knees and said, "Praise the Lord, Praise the Lord! I've got Jesus in my heart." It changes everything when Jesus comes in to stay. After the service that night, she came to us with tears in her eyes. She asked us if we wanted to know why she was weeping, "It's because I have an old grandfather and grandmother who are near death and both are blind and cannot see. They live way out in the country," she told us, and she lived with them to try and help them a little bit to get something to eat. She said, "Won't you come out and tell them about Jesus and what He'll do for them because they are near death's door?" How could we say no? We asked her to tell us the way and the next morning were off to find their home. We had to go over rice fields, and then down a little narrow path. There was no way to go even by bicycle, so we had to walk around and around maybe for two or three miles to her home where she lived with her Grandparents. As we approached, she said "We're nearing, we're nearing. I'm going to pray." Imagine, she had just accepted Jesus. She knew the worth of prayer as we did. She said, "I'm going to pray while you talk to them." We reached the place, a little bit of a shack, tumbling down and made of bamboo, and, oh, it was a miserable little place, but she showed us the way in. A little door, made it necessary for us to stoop to get into the small shack. "Where are your grandfather and grandmother?" All we saw was the immense ancestor altar, the idols of Buddha and all the other gods imaginable. We couldn't see the grandfather and grandmother. She said, "Look over in that corner, that's Grandma." She was on a bed maybe a foot from the floor, lying there blind. Then the child said, "Over there in the other corner is grandfather in another little bed." He, too, was blind.

They had never heard of Jesus. We pled with them to accept Jesus that morning, following the night that the granddaughter had been saved. We told them the way and the whole story of Jesus. They shook their heads, "Khong duoc, khong duoc" which meant no, we can't. "We must worship our ancestors. We must worship Buddha. We must bow down to all these idols and worship. No. Khong duoc." They couldn't see us, but we kept pleading with them. We must have stayed there for a couple of hours. We just couldn't persuade them to accept Jesus and went back home sad. Very sad, thinking that perhaps in a few days these two would go on not to glory, but to hell. Oh, it just made us cringe. That evening we wondered what we could do. I decided we couldn't have a sermon that night. We had to pray. We dismissed the evangelistic meeting and we spent hours, all the Christians kneeling in prayer for that old man and old woman to be saved before they died. Then at 12 o'clock, everybody just started to praise God, Praise the Lord. He'd answered prayer. The Holy Spirit came down and told us that our prayers had been answered. We went back and lay down in our little trailer with peace in our hearts and rest, not fearing anymore because we knew that God answers prayer, believing prayer.

In the morning before light, while it was still dark, we heard a knock on the door. The little girl had come in through the rice fields, followed the path to the trailer and she said, "Grandpa and Grandma are calling for you." Praise God! We went in and over to the old lady.

She took hold of Mary's arm. She said, "I can't see you. I know I can't see you, but I know you love me." Wasn't that wonderful? Isn't it wonderful to know someone loves you. The same thing happened with me and the old man. "We've changed our minds, we want to accept Jesus. We want to become Christians. We don't want to go to that bad place," they said, "we want to go up to heaven when we die." That dear old couple accepted the Lord Jesus Christ and became children of God.

Our business was *always* to be about the Lord's business of spreading the Good News to the lost people of Viet Nam.

23

Beyond Retirement

"The Alliance missionaries met in the fall of 1966 to hear reports and plan work for the coming year. The most discouraging report was concerning the closing of the boarding school for missionary children at Dalat that had served the Alliance missionaries in Southeast Asia since 1929. Grady Mangham, the Viet Nam Mission Chairman, announced that the school was reconvening at a new site in Bangkok and would be moved back to South Viet Nam when security permitted.

"Aware of anxiety in their supporting churches at home, several Alliance men presented views on the opportunities for advance in the war-ravaged country." [1] Mary and I had another furlough coming up and on September 30, 1966 wrote a letter to Rev. H. Robert Cowles, who was the Assistant to the Foreign Secretary for the C&MA (now called the Assistant Vice President for International Ministries):

We are writing to the tune of the constant roar of aircraft – helicopters, Chinooks, Sky

Raiders and cargo jets. All this accompanied by the tremendous noise of the ground travel, trucks carrying troops, and every imaginable kind of war machinery from rations, to ammunition, big guns, tanks, etc., and is interspersed by the shrill siren of a police car opening the crowded street for ambulances, fire trucks or perhaps prisoners of war. This keeps us conscious that we are in the midst of a terrible war.

Needless to say, we get weary of the awful horrors of war but God in His great mercy is daily renewing our strength, and we are witnessing by the power of the Holy Spirit a great ingathering of precious souls saved for eternity. We praise HIM for the privilege of being here "at such a time as this."

…We do extensive traveling all through the district, visiting all the churches, preaching, and witnessing all along the way. And we would not fail to thank God for journeying mercies. Many times jeeps, or other military equipment have been ambushed, as they have come in contact with mines or snipers but God has protected us by His grace and in answer to the many prayers that are going up to the throne daily for us. We praise HIM.

We have little less than a year before furlough; the Lord has been so good to us this term. Naturally we are tired of war, after 25 years of it here in Viet Nam. We long for some of the quieter years as in 1926 to 41, but they are not in sight. When we come home this time we hope to have an R&R, as the military men call it. Last furlough was hectic as you perhaps know. We suppose the District Superintendents plan their Missionary Conventions quite some time ahead so we are making a little plea, something we have not done for over 40 years. We would like to ask to be relieved from assignment on tours for perhaps six months after we arrive home next year. This will give a much needed rest instead of a 'Rush and Run' which we have experienced in the past. Our times are in His hands and we can do nothing but return to Viet Nam after furlough if the field so wishes and God wills. After all these years, we cannot disobey, His will be done! Praise Him!

We need God's answers to your prayers that we may be sustained in the midst of such awful noise and turmoil that accompanies the Qui Nhon Support Command and the 1st Calvary Division at Ankhe. They are trying to root the enemy out and clear the road north and south but it is a long tedious job. They were 'too long' digging in, it's a great mystery how after a battle the V.C.

can disappear, some to their underground haunts, and many mingle with the crowds clothed in the same garb of the peasants. The past week a furious battle was going on just eight or nine kilometers north of Qui Nhon. There were many casualties and you don't hear statistics about that. Yesterday a mine blew up a bridge not far north, now no busses or trucks can get through, but they will replace it by a temporary one soon.

It is heart breaking to go to the hospitals, and see patients lying on the floor everywhere, no room in beds, and what sights, casualties of WAR, men, women, and little children! The mother of one of our preachers was hit by a truck the day before yesterday and her leg was broken. We took her back to the refugee camp yesterday after she had to lie on the floor for 48 hours. What a wonderful Christian, never a word of complaint. We wish we could multiply our strength and time, WHAT BLESSED OPPORTUNITIES FOR SERVICE!

Rev. H. Robert Cowles responded to our letter in October 1966 saying:

Thank you for your September 30 letter. We are glad for the good news of what the Lord is doing up among the Tribes, even in the midst of the unsettled situation which is Viet Nam, 1966.

We do pray for you and the other Viet Nam missionaries regularly. We are thankful for your courage and your dedication. We are optimistic that the future will see even greater gains for the Kingdom of Christ.

We can well understand your desire for a bit of rest following this strenuous term of service. Under the new four-year arrangement for Viet Nam, the field may step up your furlough a bit from its late August date which it is now set for. As you probably know, the fall months are when we find it most difficult to secure enough missionaries to man all the tours. If there were some way for you to get home in the late spring, it is likely that we could give you the entire summer for rest in preparation for fall tour ministries. Viet Nam is much on the peoples' minds these days, and naturally missionaries from Viet Nam are much in demand on tour.

We quickly responded to Rev. Cowles letter with our concerns:

Received your letter dated October 17 and appreciate very much your consideration concerning our coming furlough.

First, allow me to make it clear what and where our work is out here. It would seem that the tribes are so prominent in the minds of people at home that some think everybody is a tribes missionary. Our work is and always has been with the Vietnamese people, 25 million of them as compared with less than a million tribes. There are practically no tribes people in Binh Dinh Province and we, Mrs. Travis and I, are the only missionaries in the midst of one million Vietnamese. You mentioned in your letter that you were 'glad for the good news of what the Lord is doing up among the Tribes.' We do praise the Lord for that but as to us, we are here swamped in war, refugees, poor wretched people who are in worse plight than any Tribesman up in the jungle safe from most of the horrors of this war. If you could have seen the 4000 Vietnamese refugees dumped on the beach here at Qui Nhon the other evening you would realize that a man in the jungle with a loin cloth as compared with these hopeless people, hungry, homeless and destitute, was fortunate. So much for that glimpse as to what is going on right around us in this wilderness of sin.

We came to this province ten years ago when it had just emerged from Communist domination. There were about 15 Christians who gathered in this town in a little rented chapel. During the last ten years we have done everything possible to reach the mass of the people in this province, open air meetings, preaching in farmers' markets with a P.A. system, living in their midst for months at a time, teaching and preaching everywhere with much house-to-house visitation. God has given a wonderful increase. One reason we are not considering an early furlough is that we are in the midst of a special evangelistic and church building program throughout the whole province. Military chaplains and Christians are enthusiastically working while the time is ripe. Unless the Lord definitely indicates, we cannot leave at this time.

Of course our term does not come under the four-year ruling and we would be disappointed to have to come home before our five years are up which is the last of August 1967. There are now eleven churches either finished or are being constructed where ten years ago there were none. In fact, five of these are finished with five more to go. Considering the contacts we have with the chaplains and nationals it would be unwise to think of leaving at this time. Perhaps we should even extend our term. The seven preachers working with us here and the

District Superintendent say that we really ought to extend and not think of leaving now.

Considering our age (Mary 74, and me 70), and the fact that we have never asked for any concession during the past forty years, and that many missionaries are given short terms, study privileges, extended furloughs for various reasons we feel that with the thought of returning to the field we should have the special consideration asked for in our last letter. There are quite a few missionaries from the fields who will be coming home early and, no doubt, will be glad to fill the need for convention work in the fall of 1967. We hope you will not suggest to this field any 'step up' as to our furlough which would complicate matters as they are now adjusting things according to the time and wishes of many missionaries. We do not wish to 'get involved.'

So, in conclusion, we would respectfully request that our furlough be not changed and that we quietly return by ship and have time for recuperation, having in mind a return to Viet Nam where we believe we are needed more than anywhere else.

P.S. We understand that the missionaries on this field are allowed a five week vacation

*out of the country but because of the pressing
needs here we don't feel we should take that
much time out with so few months left before
furlough.*

It was in the spring of 1967, we were scheduled for
furlough and retirement, our fellow-missionaries honored us with a "This is Your Life" program. Furlough
and retirement had to wait, Mary and I would plead
with the field committee to allow us to remain. There
was no replacement to send to Qui Nhon, so how could
we leave? So it was that we didn't take our furlough in
August of 1967.

24

TET Offensive of 1968

The years had carried us on and we were now several years past retirement age. Why wasn't it a good time to leave and retire? My dear wife was not interested in such plans for she had such a heart for the lost. If she saw someone walking down the road and did not know if they had heard the Good News, she would drop her head and just weep. Her heart was breaking for the lost. The harvest was so ripe and the reapers so few, how could we leave? Even as it came time for our next furlough no one could get my dear wife interested. We were booked two or three times to leave, but we were faced with such opportunities in a ripe harvest field that we felt we could not leave. We knew if we went home at our age, we would never get back and the thought made it difficult to even think about going. What momentous days from 1962 to 1975! In telling it, there is no way of exaggerating. We just try to tell it as it was.

During those years the Koreans entered the conflict. War machines, material and new modern equipment everywhere. Our equipment was the same as ever, yet new as the morning sun. Our fight was not with flesh and blood. The Holy Spirit furnished the only means that could go in and take men, women, and children for Christ that was our business. So called "close calls with death" were continually on our pathway, but eternal plans are as sure as the hand of God. Planes, helicopters, and rockets were over head most of the time. The Communists would sneak in close to the town with their rockets to be launched at night. Although in need of a little sleep after a hard day, about two o'clock we would hear fireworks begin. One night about two o'clock, we were awakened from peaceful dreams by a loud explosion. Windows and doors were blown open, such confusion there was. The back door was ripped wide open, breaking the lock; big slabs of roofing were torn off; and lights went out as the explosions continued. Their rockets had hit the American ammunition dump just a short distance from our house. The ammunition was stored on top of the ground and covered with thick layers of earth. There were dozens of these mounds of ammunition covered with dirt. The first hit set off a chain reaction and for a period of about eight hours, huge hunks of metal were flying all over town. One big piece, bigger than one's head, went through the roof of the preacher's house and landed right where he had slept the night before. We went in between two of our walls for a little more protection, stood there in the dark, looked out the back and watched all the horrible fireworks. For eight hours during the night they went on. The helicopters and gunships were soon in the air trying to get the enemy who was in the nearby jungle firing rockets. It's hard to imagine such a display. Talk about a Fourth of July fireworks show, that was something! That was just one night's experience.

There was no more sleep that night as the ammunition continued to explode and fierce gunfire was taking place all over town. Please bear with me while I take time for a special observation. During all that time my Mary stood right there with me, never murmuring, whimpering, or complaining, but just praising the Lord. She was anxious to get out the next day among the destruction and death, to try to comfort the people in the midst of such disaster. She didn't show any fear at all.

Night after night those rockets came into town and landed over in the barracks where the soldiers were and everywhere else in town. They always went over our house because we were on the edge of town near the mountains. That happened night after night, but still we were always able to get out during the day and travel throughout the country.

Even with all the turmoil no one could have foreseen or been prepared for what the North Vietnamese had planned which was the terrible offensive of 1968, called TET (the New Year attack). For those involved in the Viet Nam War, and that includes a whole generation of Americans, TET 1968 will be forever etched in our minds. For sure, TET 1968 is indelibly stamped on the minds of every missionary serving in Viet Nam at that time.[1]

At TET, people of the Orient lay aside normal responsibilities to celebrate New Year's. Fireworks and feasts celebrated the beginning of the Vietnamese New Year. It was a time of merriment and relaxation and would be a welcome truce proclaimed by the warring parties. Hopefully a holiday from horror![2]

TET '68 which began on Monday, January 29 was anything but that. The Communists had infiltrated the town in clever ways. In the weeks prior, they had staged a number of funerals and had the caskets loaded with ammunition and all sorts of war materials. When the celebrants began drifting to their homes after mid night, the Communists regrouped in cemeteries and dug up the caskets used in spurious funerals and passed out more weapons. While unsuspecting celebrants voiced the traditional TET wishes of happiness, wealth, and longevity, the Communists moved into position to attack. They had already taken over the radio station and the information bureau while everybody was having a good time and didn't know what was going on. The Communists had fooled them.

We were in our rented store building on a main street near the information bureau and the radio station. The night before the New Year's celebration there was the usual shooting fire crackers up until midnight, and then without any warning, the gunfire began. People thought it was still fire crackers, but it was the real thing.

The next morning we stepped out on the street to go to church for prayer with the Christians, which was usual on New Year's Day. Just as we started to get in the old car to go to the church, which was several blocks away, an American soldier standing behind a tree with his gun, yelled at us, "Don't go down that way; there are five Americans dead in the street already." Naturally we changed our minds and went back in to the house realizing then that God kept us there to serve Him for a few more years in Viet Nam. We then had a most horrible week, and a ringside seat to the most savage fighting, and shooting up of a big hotel to our right and the complete destruction of the radio station and information buildings, and the killing of hundreds of V.C.'s. What a gruesome sight, dead and mangled bodies everywhere.

While the Vietnamese military were out celebrating all night, the Communists burned their barracks; they were all disorganized and hopelessly confused. The Americans had all they could do to protect their airstrip and the town was practically under control of the Communists. The Korean army was about ten miles away and the only hope for the town was to call on them for help. They were soon there, with ten American tanks parked a half a block from our house, blasting away at the radio station and the information offices. The Communists had taken over all these buildings and they intended to stay there. It took six days to completely destroy those buildings and kill all the Communists who were held up inside. They were told to come out for the Koreans, but they would not. The shooting and killing all over town was fierce. Bodies were stacked up everywhere. Later they were bulldozed into piles of rubble and carted off to huge graves. What a terrible sight!

After a week, things quieted down a bit and people began to gather to see the destroyed buildings near our house. We went with the crowd to see and all at once someone in that wrecked building began shooting out. A die-hard was still in and around there refusing to surrender. It did not take the crowd long to disperse.

After things began to settle down Mary and I wrote the following in a letter to Rev. Bernard S. King, Executive Director of Funding for the C&MA (then called the Treasurer of the C&MA), dated February 28, 1968.

Although fearful days, we were glad to be here at such a time as this to rebuke sin and idolatry and point the WAY, to these poor people in distress. Even though the situation was rough, none advised us to leave, not even the head military men. Everybody was very concerned and solicitous and seemed to appreciate our staying. We hope we are not presumptuous in saying that we believe we were a boost to the morale of the people in their time of need.

It was a hard decision to make when we were told to come and be evacuated to Bangkok. To appear disobedient was a painful situation but we could not persuade ourselves to leave. We feel everyone in Qui Nhon except the V.C.'s would have been disappointed if we had left.

We marvel at God's leading that we might be able to stay and witness to the people in this awful time of distress. We were hoping and warning that there would be no fire crackers this year at 'TET' time but sad to say the uproar was worse than ever.

At this date, a month after Tet, the situation seems to be under control. Every military man is armed to the teeth and there is a curfew all night. There are some snipers, but the main force of V.C.'s have been driven out. There are terrorist attacks here and there but we are O.K. as long as our steps are ordained by the Lord. We don't get much sleep because of the continued roar of guns through the night but we are now able to travel in the daytime. At night everything is buttoned up, patrols are everywhere and everybody is wishing for morning."

In his book, *By Life or By Death*, James C. Hefley recounted the details of the war after visiting the Viet Nam field and many of the surviving missionaries. He made the following notes concerning us: "One Alliance couple, the C.E. (Chester) Travises, spent every night of TET week on the floor of their home.

"The Travises were the senior C&MA missionaries in Viet Nam. After the city's biggest battle was fought only a block-and-a-half from their house, the U.S. military offered to evacuate them. 'No,' Chester Travis declared. 'We've been in Viet Nam almost 50 years. We're needed now more than ever.' "

In actuality, TET 1968 was a signal victory for the Allies. Few ever really appreciated that. During all the preceding years, there had been large numbers of "closet" communists throughout South Viet Nam. During the TET Offensive these locals were so sure of instant victory that they stepped out into the streets with their guns blazing. And when they started shooting, the American army, the Vietnamese army, and the Korean army killed them all.

The TET Offensive struck more than 100 cities and towns, even the center of Saigon. In some areas the fighting raged for four weeks, inflicting heavy losses on the Communists, who were defeated. The Communists lost thousands of soldiers; most of them were local Viet Cong. After that, V.C. activity dropped like a spent rocket. From then on, the war was strictly outside intervention from the North. But the TET Offensive galvanized the United States civilians' attitude against an already unpopular war. In fact, what was a stunning defeat for North Viet Nam ironically marked the beginning of North Viet Nam's triumph.

For The Christian and Missionary Alliance, TET 1968 resulted in the largest single loss of missionaries since the 1910 Boxer Rebellion in China. Five missionaries – Ed Thompson and his wife Ruth (Stebbins) Thompson, Carolyn Griswold, Ruth Wilting, Robert Ziemer – plus Carolyn's visiting father, Leon Griswold, died as the Viet Cong overran the Mission property on the outskirts of Ban Me Thuot. A C&MA Leprosarium worker, Betty Olsen, as well as Wycliffe missionary Henry Blood, and a civilian forestry expert, Mike Benge, were taken captive.

Betty Olsen and Henry Blood died in the jungle of starvation and disease many months later. Mike Benge was eventually released several years later and returned to the States.[3]

Mary and I expressed our regards to the bereaved C&MA families from the TET attack in the letter we had written to Rev. Bernard S. King:

Our hearts are deeply saddened by the home-going of our beloved missionaries at Ban Me Thuot. We first heard the news over F.E.B.C. Manila while we were in the midst of the uproar of war in the streets of Qui Nhon. How our hearts ached for the friends and loved ones they had left behind. May the God of all comfort be with them.

They've run their course, they've reached their goal
At home now with the Lord,
And there with Him they now receive
Their Saviour's rich reward.

Well done, thou faithful servant mine,
Come now rejoice with Me
In all the joys of your new home
Forever here set free.

By faith, O Holy Comforter
For dear ones so bereaved,
Just let them see their loved ones safe
In Heaven's joy received.

They heard the call and went with Him,
And soon they will return,
With all the many tribes redeemed
For this great day we yearn.

We listen for the trumpet sound
For His return we pray,
When He shall come with loved ones dear
And wipe all tears away.

The TET destruction and the Ban Me Thuot killings aroused some home supporters to plead that missionaries leave Viet Nam because of the danger.[4] But few would leave. Dr. Louis L. King, Vice President for International Ministries of C&MA (then called the Foreign Secretary), met with some of the missionaries. He noted the Travis' stubbornness with regards to leaving the field. "As the Alliance's senior missionaries in Viet Nam with 48 years of service, they were past retirement and had not been home for furlough in almost seven years. Dr. King suggested they should return to the U.S. Both said 'No! The opportunities are too great for us to think of leaving so soon.'

"Later in June Dr. King asked them when they would be coming home so speaking engagements in churches could be set up. 'It would be nice to go on furlough,' Mr. Travis replied, 'but we still can't think of leaving.'"

It seemed the sentiments of the remaining missionaries on the Viet Nam field were best spoken by missionary Eugenia Johnston who said, "If we can't trust the Lord for our lives – for either death or life – how dare we try to tell those who know nothing about Him that they can trust Him?"[5]

The Lord had His hand of protection on us and we still were not interested in leaving. Even though that year the people in Viet Nam saw and heard more fireworks than they wanted.

The Harvest Is Wasting

The harvest is ripe and wasting,
Reapers are needed today,
The call for help is so urgent
For ones who will go and pray.

Do not wait till time's no more
The opportune time all past,
Now is the day of salvation
This joyous privilege won't last.

Think, there never again will be
A time of reaping like this,
And through all those endless ages
The purpose of life we miss.

We may cry for another chance
But our cry will not avail,
'Tis now the harvest is passing
To wait, is only to fail.

Let's follow the Lord of the harvest
Let our eyes see what He sees,

He will open our ears today
And through Him we'll hear their pleas.

The cry of the millions out there
They are helpless, hopeless, LOST,
To fail to tell them of Jesus
Entails a horrible cost.

There'll be nothing laid up in Glory
When earthly riches are past,
Only the ones we've helped to save
Are the treasures that will last.

So let us go forth a weeping
While bearing that precious seed,
Then doubtless we will come again
With the harvest, and joy indeed.

Then through all the endless ages
We will be so glad we gave,
All that we have and are
Perishing millions to save.

25

Final Years

In April 1968 we wrote a letter to our Field Chairman Grady Mangham saying:

About furlough, it doesn't seem to be the Lord's plan for us to leave soon...God has done wonderful things for which we praise Him, but the needs are tremendous, and so many souls are dying without Christ! It seems that we shall be pretty well tied up for some time to come. We have not had time to think about coming home... Since the Lord has so graciously kept us, and given us the health to continue, we feel that we should stay on perhaps till spring 1969. We know our children will be disappointed, but they will forgive and patiently wait as the Lord leads.

The guns are booming night and day and jets are dropping bombs many times rattling our doors and windows. The Koreans and Americans are scorching the earth in a terrific drive just north of town, having finally decided to clean out the constant threat to Qui Nhon. It doesn't seem that much news gets out from here. Perhaps the reporter is not on his job if there is one here.

With all the scrounging for building materials, carting, grading, etc, as well as all the constant demands from all the preachers throughout the province, the regular trips, and the sad condition of the OLD MERCURY we are kept well occupied.

During these last years of seed sowing and harvest, twelve new churches were built in that one province of one million people. As always, from the great number saved during the constant open air gatherings, young Vietnamese men and women were ready to go to Bible school and prepare for the ministry. That's the way the new churches that were springing up everywhere were taken care of as we moved on into new fields to reap the harvest. Viet Nam which had been a closed country little known by the rest of the world, was now in the spot light and was causing such turmoil in the United States. There was no end to the killing, and with the stall tactics America was using, there was no end to the war. The only thing good about it all was that we could stay on as long as things did not completely fall apart but it was fast coming to that conclusion. Although the storm was at its fiercest we could do nothing but continue to snatch poor people as "brands from the burning." (Jude 23)

Mary continued her letter writing and poems to the children. She sent Evangel a special Happy Birthday poem on February 9, 1969:

Time and distance cannot change our love for you, dear
Only make it grow and deepen every day.
How we'd love to be with you our darling daughter
To express it in a satisfactory way.

Seems like yesterday we held you in our arms, dear
With our hearts aflame with love and joy, and pride.
Oh, what joy now fills our hearts as we look forward
Once again to have you darling by our side.

Testing, trials, tears and sorrow cannot daunt us
For we have our Saviour's promise tried and true.
He will change the tears to diamonds on the mountain
Our experience in the valley will be through.

May His presence ever be your joy and comfort
As you praise Him for His blessings 'long the way.
Happy Birthday, precious daughter, how we love you
Soon we'll tell you face to face, OH HAPPY DAY!

We were again scheduled for furlough and were bid farewell but it was always the same story; with so many souls hanging in the balance we could not get interested in any "means of transportation to America," which we knew would be the last. The situation was becoming so bad that many plans were made for evacuation by the United States military. Communist infiltration was being carried on so cleverly that no one realized how serious it really was. No one could tell who were Communist and who were South Vietnamese.

It was during these years that Tom Stebbins became our Field Chairman and we worked more closely with him. Tom later shared some of his memories during that time, "Some years later, at age 36, I was elected to serve as Viet Nam Field Chairman. Chester and Mary could have viewed my young, inexperienced leadership with disdain, but no, never did they ever treat me with anything but love, humility, and respect. This exemplary attitude was put to a significant test when, one day the national leaders summoned me to the Binh Dinh province to deal with a conflict that had arisen between their local pastors and the Travises. Being just one year older than their youngest son Urb, I found this assignment extremely difficult. After the pastors stated clearly their complaint, Chester and Mary presented their side of the story. Apologies and regrets were expressed on both sides as the meeting closed with tears, laughter and hugs. It was a magnificent demonstration of the poverty of spirit and meekness, which Jesus our Lord, centuries earlier, had set forth clearly in His beatitudes. Is it any wonder then that He blessed this Christ-like pioneer missionary couple right up to their last days of service for Him?"

It was in 1969, President Nixon pressed the military for "Vietnamization" of the conflict. This meant improving training and arming of South Viet Nam's military, which was to take a larger role in defending the country. It also involved the withdrawal of forces. Nixon hoped to limit U.S. casualties, but bloody battles continued.

Each year there was a report made covering each mission district for the Alliance. The following note was later put in the C&MA Archive file as the concluding page of Viet Nam's narrative report for 1969. Arni Shareski sent a note to H. Robert Cowles saying, "not being too poetical at heart I'm unable to evaluate the poem but the sentiment seems quite good. Obviously, Tom Stebbins is referring to Rev. and Mrs. C.E. Travis." Tom had finished his report writing:

"Perhaps the spirit of our missionary staff in Viet Nam is best expressed by one elderly missionary couple who continue to labor in a province of one million people, several years past retirement, and in their ninth year without furlough. When asked why they wouldn't go home, they responded:

We're tired of turmoil, sin and war
The night has been so long,

Yet when we turn our steps toward home
There comes a voice so strong.

We turn and look, what do we see?
A scene that breaks our heart,
The hopeless millions waiting still
So how can we depart?

The helpless broken throng our way,
They still in darkness grope,
How can we leave them in despair
Without one ray of hope?

That sea of faces sick and sad
Loom up before our eyes,
How can we turn and leave for home
Amidst these plaintive cries?

So though the homeland beckons still
We cannot break away,
But "throw the line" and carry on
While you hold on and pray.

During that time the mission headquarters called from Saigon and reached us through the American military, telling us to leave for Saigon. We asked if those were official orders or just advice. Anyway, we did not hear any more from Saigon and found out we could not get out of town if we wanted to. Strange to say, we were happy that there was no way out.

That was six years before we had to finally leave the people we had learned to love. Isn't it strange to be so thankful for the privilege of staying in such a mess? It was God's doing, so wonderful in our eyes. From the night of TET 1968 on, the gates to the town were closed. VC would come out on the road and put mines there at night so when we started out in the daytime, we didn't know what would happen. They would choose who they wanted to blow up, I guess. Sometimes it would be automatic and other times it would be by someone hiding off in the field with a string or an electric connection to blow it up. When we'd go along the road in the morning, we'd see trucks loaded with pigs all blown up. The saddest thing was when it hit a bus load of people. They would be scattered along the road, blown to pieces, torn up, poor frightened individuals. We would stop and do all we could to help. What an experience our divine assignment was and for such a purpose!

Now we had to travel during the day, going to visit the churches and the market places along the way with the same old story that we loved and had preached for nearly 50 years. That same power of God was bringing poor, scared, hopeless people to know Jesus. All knew we were there for one purpose and that we were neutral. It is not altogether a bleak picture there. How we praise God that we could travel freely, everybody knew our old car, and recognized us. They say: "Tin Lành, Ong Ba Tin lành" (Mr. & Mrs. Good News) and they sometimes add "Ong Ba thuong chung toi" (our Grandparents love us). In Viet Nam they lovingly refer to anyone who was old as Grandma or Grandpa. How wonderful to love and be loved! We had a sign on our car that read, *Tin lành* meaning Good News or "Gospel," along with the symbol of the C&MA and the National Evangelical Church.[1] Everyone knew who we were but they couldn't understand why anyone from America could be so foolish to spend their lives out there, helping those people under such distress. A couple of "old birds" running around among those people was peculiar. People would ask a lot of questions about why we stayed there, and we would tell them, "The love of Christ constrains us; we can't do anything different." (2 Corinthians 5:14) To give up and go home earlier than we absolutely had to would have been miserable. To consider being back in the United States and sitting around there thinking of the land of Viet Nam that was our home for years made us sad. We were glad to be able to stay and the Vietnamese were listening to the Gospel as never before. Praise the Lord!

Young men by the thousands were being carved up in the jungle, not only the Americans, but the Vietnamese as well. As we traveled along the road we would sometimes see a mile or two of trucks loaded with soldiers.

We had thousands of tracts and Gospels of John and we'd try to give one to each of the soldiers.

The poor Vietnamese were on their way, never to come back. We saw the Americans in a little different way. We'd go to the airport where they lived in barracks. We'd visit them and preach to them, but our time was really for the Vietnamese. That's what we were there for. The Americans could know the Gospel if they wanted to. They had their chaplains.

Throughout 1970, U.S. forces steadily withdrew, but U.S. air power continued to support the South Vietnamese. Another year had rolled around and Mary again wrote a poem to Evangel on February 9, 1970.

God gives the sunshine
God gives the rain,
God gives the harvest's
Ripe golden grain.

God gave you, too, Evangel dear
To make our joy complete,
A precious darling daughter
So loving and so sweet.

We love you, our own girlie;
We love to have you near.
We'd give a million dollars
If you were only here.

But while we wait for orders
To hasten home to you,
We'll pray for one another
And to our Lord be true.

Some day we'll hear the trumpet
Our Lord will come again,
We'll meet with Him in glory
No separation then.

We were ready for another break when we joined in the Annual Mission Conference for The Christian & Missionary Alliance that year. Few of us delegates even realized it was Viet Nam's 50th Mission Conference that was in session. Except for Mary and myself, none of the other delegates were even born when the first Mission Conference was first convened in 1920. One of the highlights of the 1970 C&MA Mission Conference was also the celebration of our 50th Wedding Anniversary. We were the "senior citizens" of the Viet Nam Mission Field.[2]

Chester & Mary Travis
Golden Wedding Day
April 22, 1970

Content with you, though far from home
And children we love so dear,

My love for you grows greater far
Throughout each passing year.

'Tis love, sweetheart that made us one
Long fifty years ago,
'Tis love that fills our hearts today
And keeps them all aglow.

Through thick and thin our precious Lord
Has bound our hearts together,
And given grace to meet the trials
In every kind of weather.

Christ's love is boundless Oh so great
He's led us all the way,
And showered blessings from above
As we, His will obey.

The future's bright as on we go
Our Captain leading on,
Our one desire to win more souls
Before our work is done.

And now we thank you blessed Lord
For all these years You've given,
For precious souls saved by thy Grace
And on their way to heaven.

The next year on April 11, 1971, Mary wrote a
letter to our oldest son, Jonathan and his wife Ruth

updating them on what our days had been like. It had been another long and tiring year and she wrote, "we have really been on the run these days, ready to fall in bed when night comes, sometimes too it is not very early, we had two evening meetings, I had to get a message for the Women's Meeting Wednesday evening, and the three churches here in Qui Nhon had a joint meeting Thursday evening, quite an affair, church full. Then every day, the order of the day is callers, sometimes with S.O.S. calls that we have to run to immediately. It's good to be busy but we surely do have to call on the Lord for added strength. Continue to pray for us ...Oh, for an end of this awful war which is bringing such suffering."

It was also in 1971 that our son Paul and his wife Ruth came out for a visit. We had not seen any of our children since 1962 on our last furlough. Paul was the only one of our children that was ever able to make the trip back to Viet Nam after leaving as a child. While there Paul was able to visit many of the places he had been as a child, where he was born in Nha Trang, and meet the young lady who had cared for him as a baby.

Paul later described an incident that occurred on the road one day while visiting Viet Nam, "We were driving down the road in the midst of the war going on all around us. My mother had a driver's license, but never drove anywhere because my dad was always with her. Dad was driving with Mother sitting beside him and she had her right arm resting on the door with her elbow out the window. This is the way they always sat in the car. We passed a burning bus on one side that had been blown up and you could see the fighting down in the valley below. I asked Dad if we were turning back. 'No, we'll just wait; it will pass soon,' was his casual response. There was gun fire back and forth across the road and then an armed man shot his gun right over the front of the car. Dad floored it and we drove right past him. Ruthie and I 'hit the deck' in the back seat of the car to get out of the firing line. When I looked up, both Mom and Dad were sitting in their same positions, just as though nothing had happened! When I asked Dad, 'What was that?' his casual reply was, 'Target practice,' then added, 'Don't you know you're immortal till your work is done?'"

That was an experience for Paul and Ruth as they were not used to the war days of Viet Nam and had come to visit us partly, to try and convince us to leave there. By this time we were many years past retirement age and nearly ten years since having a furlough.

After Paul and Ruth's visit we wrote a letter to express our gratitude to the Pineville Alliance Church who had helped them make their trip possible. We shared how much the visit had meant to us. "It was such a blessing to us and they really enjoyed seeing what God is doing here as well as having the opportunity to minister to the Viet Nam church here and also at the big

Phu Cat Airbase twenty-five miles from here and at the International Church at Saigon. We did not like to have them go but duty calls and they had to return to work in their part of the Harvest Field where God has called them. Separation is the hardest part of Missionary work but just a little longer and we'll be together forever. Praise the Lord! Thanks a million for making their visit possible."

We wrote to our Field Chairman, Tom Stebbins in April 1971 giving him an update on what we had been doing, "Just night before last we got one of the worst rocket attacks yet... That horrible explosion was when a rocket hit an ammunition dump that had 500 pound bombs. This dump was not more than two hundred yards from this camp. Everything there was a tangled mess. Houses all around were wrecked and the building that stored the bombs was nothing but a huge black spot, nothing left. Some of the ceiling was torn loose in our house, it has taken quite a bit of time to get things back together but it is wonderful that no major damage was done to the house. We thank the Lord for that. The locks and hinges I have repaired. If we had had glass windows in the house they would have all been broken. Thanks for your prayers and God's safe keeping that we might continue to witness for Him here."

Carrying on with her letter writing, Mary wrote a note to Paul and his wife Ruth in October, 1971 saying,

"Dad gets pretty tired, he just won't stop to rest, and he has lost a lot of weight. Mom too has thinned down a bit. Guess that's O.K. It is hard to sleep well *[ngu ngon]* and *an ngon* [eat well] when we see so many suffering. We are glad you are praying for us."

In my 1971 Qhi Nhon report I wrote:

> *The curtain has dropped; the scenes of 1971 are gone, but our memory still pictures the awful tragedies of the past year. Another chapter is written and so much is in red, the blood of poor dying men everywhere. How we would like to get away from it all, but with such a message of hope for a lost world how can we leave? The beauties of earth and sky shine through the darkness in spite of the vileness of man. The marvelous thing is God's infinite love for these poor people which eclipses everything else in the world. Underneath His love, we carry on with joy unspeakable and full of glory. Praise His Name!*

> *How we do thank and praise Him for health and daily strength and the privilege of telling others of the abundant life there is in Christ Jesus our Lord. In the midst of such horrible scenes everywhere God is doing great things in answer to the prayers of His people for Viet Nam.*

Many events of the past year may seem important, astronauts on the moon, great scientific discoveries, etc. Such things fade before the 'joy in His presence of the angels over one sinner that repenteth.' How good it has been to be in on the thing that brings the greatest joy to the heart of our wonderful Lord!

"Soliciting help from man is futile, which we have avoided. But we have coveted the prayers of God's people everywhere for an old time revival. The response has been wonderful and the answers are coming. Praise the Lord! 'Mercy drops are falling all around us but for the showers we plead.' We believe God is longing to bring a great awakening to the church in Viet Nam, without which all our efforts will come to naught.

'Time and tide waiteth for no man.' In Binh Dinh province we have seen the tide of American military power come and now it is fast going out, and will soon be all gone perhaps except military advisors...

To be able to travel throughout Binh Dinh Province with the Wonderful Word of Life during this past year is marvelous in our eyes. That doors are wide open and people so receptive to

*the Good News is truly all of God's grace. How
can a land so many years in war still be open to
the Gospel? It is something out of this world,
and truly from Heaven. By His grace may we see
that revival we have so needed all these years,
without which the church and Viet Nam will go
down in defeat.*

The Communists were still there. Fighting was still
going on everywhere. With hardly a night of sleep, we
were awakened at all hours of the night as the rockets,
mortars and endless gunfire could be heard all around,
along with helicopters overhead at all hours. It really
did get wearisome, to say the least. The Communists
were feverishly preparing for another offensive and everybody was on their toes, ready to go further South
where they thought they might be safer. You see, the
province we were working in for those years had been
so brainwashed that great numbers of the people were
sympathetic with the Communists, so people thought
that to go south was safer.

Such fear, such hopeless despair everywhere, and
what an opportune time to reach them with the only
hope there is in the world, Jesus. The people were fleeing for their lives without a ray of hope anywhere. The
war did help to destroy a lot of ancestor altars though.
Those ancestor altars went to pieces with everything else

when the bombs dropped. Then the people weren't worried about the ancestor altars, they wanted to save their lives. No doubt the Lord allowed this conflict to jar people loose from their set ways. He simply tore up that country. It's just like plowing the field, overturning it. It's only then that you can plant the seed. In spite of the war, we wouldn't have missed those years for anything.

26

Our Time's Up

We praised the Lord that it was four years before the V.C.'s tried anything like TET again. This time they had not infiltrated the town, but were organizing out in the country for a real invasion. This invasion was a failure, and the town was saved for our final round of two more years pioneering into the thick jungle of the hearts of people throughout that dark region of Viet Nam.

It was now 1972. People heard that a host of Communists were approaching the town, determined to take over. Panic ruled the town, everybody was frantically searching for ways to get out and head for the south. "Perfect love casteth out fear," but so few knew that love, so they latched onto any vehicle they could find and hit the road. In the wild rush they had no end of trouble, wrecking cars and trucks through the mountain passes and over the bridges, fleeing the wrath of the Communists. Oh that men might learn to flee the wrath of God against SIN! Well, the Lord had a few more years for us in Viet Nam and how glad we are we did not run!

No, there was no danger and the Lord was so good, we didn't seem to have any sense of fear. I guess it was sort of strange that we'd go along the road and had no thought that at any minute the road might blow up under us. We didn't give it any thought whatsoever. As we went along one day we heard a rifle shot and the tire went flat. I thought it was the tire that made the noise. When I got up to a place where I could change the tire; put on a new one or patch the hole and pump it up, I heard something rattling inside the tube. What was it? I had to get it out, and finally discovered it was a bullet. Someone shot at us but hit the tire instead. We had all kinds of these experiences – they are too numerous to recall.

One day, right at noon, I stepped out of the house, and zoom! Right over my head, not 50 feet above was a rocket that landed downtown just where we used to live. It hit exactly where the old car had been parked. There it killed five people. What a fierce sounding thing as it went over my head. Those rockets just whiz over and roar on the way.

It was getting difficult to simply carry on with daily tasks. During this time, Mary shared in a letter to the children, "Mom is up to her old tricks again this morning, four o'clock and I woke up at three o'clock and after praying for you all, I couldn't seem to go to sleep so

I reckoned I'd better write to you. It has been kind of noisy at night, lots of loud talk, guns and one wonders what is going on, the dog is also barking, he is on a leash and has access to the whole yard, and seems to think he must take care of us. I have brought the typewriter out in the dining room so as not to keep Dad awake, he got to sleep late for his supper kind of upset him. I have put some bread in the oven to make some hard toast too in order to save the bread. We like hard toast, it keeps well.

"It continues to rain, the water was coming up in our yard the other day but yesterday it was sunny all morning and we got a big wash out and dry, we were very fortunate for we had been getting along washing a few things by hand and drying them in the open garage. Guess the rains will continue another month, hope without typhoon winds.

"My hard toast is done, the woman has come in to start cleaning up for Sunday, and Dad is up shaving so I guess I will make some coffee and get a bite to reinforce my strength for the day. How I would like to see you this morning. I get so lonesome for you all."

Now 1974 it had been twelve long years without a change or furlough and we were long past retirement age at 81 and 76. We began to realize it was getting late in the afternoon of our stay in the midst of those dear folks we so love. At 76 years of age, getting little sleep, with the constant fighting and destruction everywhere,

I didn't need any diet pills to begin to lose weight; I was soon down from my normal weight of 170 lbs. to 150 lbs. We were getting really tired. All those years were constant turmoil, hardly ever having a full night's sleep because of all the noise from the rockets exploding nearby. Friends and family were urging us to take off for home. Viet Nam was our home. How could we leave? They would book us by air, but we kept stalling, giving little thought about packing up. It seemed strange that we had little inclination for the trip to that great land of America we had seen so little of since 1925.

In August 1974, Vice President Ford replaced Nixon, who had resigned after a political blunder. Congress and most Americans were weary of the Viet Nam War, so the United States now refused to defend South Viet Nam. The South Vietnamese knew they had been abandoned by America – their morale was crushed[1].

The Americans were gone and the worst turmoil and chaos of all the years was erupting. We knew if we stayed it would mean getting captured. The darkness of night was closing in fast. Things were falling to pieces and there was danger on every side. A Vietnamese girl who was helping us out went over one day to get some water from the well. She found two big bottles that were empty. Arsenic had been poured into the well. She could have drunk it but the Lord prevented her from doing so. We were always conscious of the Lord's protection and never really felt the danger.

We were able to attend the last missionary conference at Dalat, having obtained a free ride aboard an American military plane. We had a blessed time together, not realizing how near we all were to the end of any more missionary work.

Every memory brings a tear,
As we leave Viet Nam so dear.

Here where ties have grown so strong,
As we've mingled with the throng.

From which thousands born of love,
By God's message from above.

Bound in fellowship so sweet,
Everywhere we go we meet.

Roots so deep in this dear land,
Midst these friends we understand.

As we've walked through toil and tears,
God had kept us through the years.

By His plan which is so good,
In His grace we've understood.

By God's love constrained to stay,
Even though so hard the way.

Seeking souls, what a treasure,
In His glory without measure.

Treasures there laid up above,
For the One we dearly love.

Our dear Lord now leads us on,
Each hour nearer to the dawn.

As we go hearts left behind,
In our Lord we'll comfort find.

There we'll hold the line each day,
As for them we work and pray.

Those were our final words we shared at that last missionary conference at Dalat in 1974. We hurried back to our station, thanks to the kindness of a military plane giving us our last air view of that beautiful land, marred only by the war and sin. We had gotten word that there was finally a ship, the *U.S.S. President Grant*, with one cabin left, so all systems were go and the count down for our departure began. Tom Stebbins insisted we sail on now. Departure was upon us. Over five decades of mission work was drawing to an abrupt close.

We had just a few days left before loading drums and trunks on an old truck headed for Saigon. Each day was heart-breaking as our dear friends known through the years came to say goodbye. The Lord eased the pain by giving new friends right on the spot before leaving. As we were loading to go, the girl who had been around helping so much came in and, on her knees before my wife, began to cry so bitterly, saying she would not see her anymore. Mary put her arms around her and said, "We can be together forever if you'll accept Jesus," and right there she did just that, praying to Jesus. She was from a Buddhist family, but found the joy of the Lord in those last minutes before we left. Praise the Lord!

Then there was the old mechanic who was always around to help me keep the old car running. In those same last moments he said about the same thing, but I assured him we could be together forever with Jesus. "Just bow your head and accept Jesus right now," I said and with tear-filled eyes we prayed together. What joy to see the working of the Spirit of God right down to the last moments! Oh, how painful to have to leave, but God knew best what we should do. We had finished the course fully assured that it was His plan for us to move out. The churches planted were His; He would jealously take care of them all. He said, *"I will build My church; and the gates of hell shall not prevail against it."* (Matthew 16:18)

We had loaded boxes and barrels with our earthly goods, then put them on an old truck. Since we were delayed in saying farewell to our loved ones; we told the truck driver to go on ahead to the ship in Saigon. We followed behind in the old Falcon which we had had the privilege of wearing out for the Lord. It was a long trip to Saigon in that fragile old vehicle over some awful war-torn roads. We soon developed radiator trouble, but were able to fix that and still keep up with the truck.

By nightfall we had made it to a town called Phan Rang, bringing back wonderful memories when we used to work in that district. This was about halfway to Saigon. The most dangerous part of the trip was still ahead. We got an early start, hoping to get to Saigon before night. For miles we traveled through familiar territory where we had spread the Good News over a period of fifty years. We could not help but drop tears along the way. Soon the road took us into the deep jungle with fierce fighting on both sides. The roads were constructed so we had to go up, across, and down. Along the way we had to cross the firing line between the North and South Vietnamese. We couldn't stop or turn back because this was the last ship and our only chance to get to America. Bridges had been wrecked and temporary ones constructed to take their place. We came to a bridge crudely made of rough planks that had been quickly bolted together to accommodate military trucks. We got over this one, but a soldier yelled saying, "Your gas tank is leaking!" I jumped out and took a look at a situation which seemed hopeless. Something we hit on the bridge put a hole in the gas tank out there in the middle of the shooting war, in the middle of nowhere, with no hope of help to come from anywhere around. The truck had gone on ahead and there we were with gas running out of the tank.

What could we do? We needed to catch that truck before the tank was empty! So we stepped on it. Gas was streaming near the exhaust pipe. For about twenty miles we did not stop to view the scenery or pay any attention to the soldiers shooting across the road. We had to catch that truck so they could pull us to where we could get gas and repair the leak. Soon we saw the truck with all our belongings ahead and zoomed past just as the old car sputtered its last. No more gas. Well, they happened to have a piece of web about ten feet long with which to pull the car.

Following so closely, tied to that old lumbering buggy ahead, was a hair-raising experience. It was about fifty miles before we reached any place that had gas. But what good is gas if it is going to run out as fast as you put it in? We finally stuffed the hole with rags and then made paste out of soap and plastered it on thick. Gasoline does not dissolve soap and we were glad for that. That done, we put in just enough gas to get us to Saigon and were off, trusting the patch to hold the rest of the way.

About six o'clock we pulled up to the dock where we had first landed more than 50 years before. The ship we were booked on, the *U.S.S. President Grant*, was to leave in three days. All earthly treasures were soon loaded into a big container on the dock and hoisted on the ship, but our real treasures, were the dear people we were leaving behind—all those precious souls we had gathered through the years. Many were still on earth, but so many more had gone on before, and are waiting to "receive us in those mansions that never perish." Glory to our precious Lord!

It seemed so strange that after all those years of turmoil that our departure was quiet. We departed our beloved Viet Nam in February of 1975. I praise the Lord for all those years, even in opposition and wars, we were there and the Lord somehow kept the doors open right down to the very end. From 1927, when the church was first organized there and the Bible had been translated, there was the challenge to have God's Book under my arm and go out with it. We had an open door up until 1974, then it was time we turned everything over to the nationals.

Our ship departed and it was several hours down that river to the ocean. What a heart-breaking trip! As we thrust out into the sea, we took our last look back to that land so dear to our hearts. What could we do? Just stand there and cry. The ship stopped at many ports on the way across the Pacific, but our hearts were far behind back in Viet Nam. It felt like six weeks of tears sailing to the U.S.A. The Lord had to keep reminding us that it was His church, His people, and that He would carefully guard His own and we would be with them again on that great day of His return.

In a lightning-fast battle, the North Vietnamese Army swept through South Viet Nam, capturing Saigon. This campaign ended almost 30 years of continuous fighting in Viet Nam. On April 30, 1975 South Viet Nam capitulated. The dark cover of communism was now spread over all of Viet Nam.

For we would not, brethren, have you ignorant of our trouble which came to us in Asia, that we were pressed out of measure, above strength, insomuch that we despaired even of life: but we had the sentence of death in ourselves, that we should not trust in ourselves, but in God which raiseth the dead... Ye also helping together by prayer for us, that for the gift bestowed upon us by the means of many persons thanks may be given by many on our behalf. (2 Corinthians 1:8-9, 11)

27

The Upward Call

After 40-some days, the old crate glided into Los Angeles harbor. What a day when we finally met up with our children and grandchildren on the West Coast whom we had not seen in 14 years! After being gone for over 50 years, many of my first thoughts were summed up with this poem:

When Loss is Gain

The way to sin is just to lose
And never try your way to choose

There's only One who knows the way
A faithful guide from day to day

Count all you've gained as so much loss
And with your Lord take up your cross

What others do what's that to thee?
For Jesus says, "Just follow Me"

Forgetting things that are behind
And live with Him Who is so kind

Make Jesus Christ your living goal
He'll give you joy down in your soul

Press toward that mark He's set for you
Then He will lead and see you through

He'll give you life that has no end
And be your everlasting friend

'Tis then you'll see how loss is gain
With Him in His eternal reign.

We were too young to settle down so we bought a motor home to travel in. I was only 79 years old and Mary a young 83! We traveled to the C&MA Council that year and then on to Maine to visit Mary's family. Mary had left Maine during WWI and was now back to visit in her twilight years around 60 years later. We spent the summer of 1975 there, then back to California to continue visiting our children scattered all over the state. We also traveled and spoke in churches, giving them the update on what was happening in Viet Nam. We always wanted to be sharing the message of the need for constant prayer for the church in Viet Nam.

How could we ever sum up our years in Viet Nam in a short message to the congregations? We continued to share our message, "I would like to be a little presumptuous and speak about the urgent need of prayer for Viet Nam. You don't hear much about it, and sometimes folks at home think we had it made out there, that the church is doing fine and everything is going well. But the church in Viet Nam is just like the church at home. Unless there is much prayer backing, it can't go forward. As far as reaching the millions in Viet Nam, it will never be done unless there's a real upward surge in this prayer effort." That was our plea.

From place to place, we shared of our travels in Viet Nam when the G.I's were there in full force. We'd go down to the airstrip and get on anything that flew, taking a trip here and there, and always going out to preach the Gospel. We would get on one of those C-123's. The whole thing roars as if it were falling to pieces. Soon it goes right up and then we were in the sky wondering how it would hold together. The crew would see us two old birds on board and take us up into the cockpit to sit where we could see things just as they were going on. Down below in the belly of the plane, the G.I.'s were squeezed in with no comfort of any kind. There they couldn't see out, but we had a full view from where the pilots sat. Sometimes the privilege was downright embarrassing.

The point we always wanted to make was that "Jesus wants us to come up with Him to see what He sees. And when we do that, it will change our lives completely. We will know how to pray – not so much in knowing how to pray as to have a deep burden to intervene for the lost." That was the message we tried to share as we toured from church to church after our return from Viet Nam. Prayer was so urgent especially now as the Communist curtain was drawn over Viet Nam.

On August 1, 1975, the C&MA Division of Overseas Ministries officially placed us on full retiral status on the basis of 50 years and five months of continuous service. We received a letter with those details from Arni Shareski, the Assistant to the Vice-President of International Ministries for the C&MA. He wrote, "Surely there is a great multitude of people in Southeast Asia who are now in the kingdom of God because of your faithful ministering to them the light of the Gospel. We shall be praying that the Lord will give you yet many years of enjoyable retiral ministries for Him."[1]

On one occasion after our return to California, Paul and our daughter-in-law Ruth took us out to eat over in Concord, California, to a Vietnamese Restaurant. It was quite a drive to get there but it was the only Vietnamese Restaurant Paul and Ruth could find in the area. Paul recalls the event and being so amazed, "When my dad walked into that restaurant, he and the guy working there took one look at each other and immediately began chatting. Obviously they were friends from Viet Nam. With the little Vietnamese language I knew, I picked up on the story; the man had become a helicopter pilot while the Americans were in Viet Nam.

He was somehow able to get a hold of a helicopter and loaded his family. He flew the helicopter and crashed it on the deck of an American aircraft carrier. The helicopter was a loss, they pushed it over board and the family then had their ride to America. It was incredible how my dad knew Vietnamese people everywhere he went."

After traveling and visiting our family some, we finally thought we might need a home somewhere so we found a nice little cottage in Castro Valley, which is in the San Francisco Bay Area of California. Paul and his family lived close by. Such happy days we had living quietly together and reaching out by prayer across that vast expanse of ocean, touching the people who are now in such fires and testing. How good to have had the privilege of planting the Church on such a sure foundation, God's Word, so that *"the gates of hell shall not prevail against it."* (Matthew 16:18)

"Fear thou not; for I am with thee: be not dismayed; for I am thy God, I will strengthen thee; yea, I will help thee; yea, I will uphold thee with the right hand of my righteousness." (Isaiah 41:10)

As I recall the strange ways the Lord led during those years of war in Viet Nam, one of the most remarkable things was how God relieved us of fear. Fear and the instinct for self-preservation is so normal, yet as I remember those days it did not occur to us that we should be afraid. We did not seem to realize what the situation was, yet we knew that the province of over a million people had been under North Vietnamese communist rule for over 15 years and most of the people were brainwashed and sympathetic with the North Vietnamese. They say ignorance is bliss, yet we really know they hated America and the South Vietnamese government. Still I now wonder why we would have gone with our camp trailer outfit to live in among them in the open for months at a time without any fear. It never occurred to us that any night they might tear us to pieces and leave no trace of what had happened. They could have wiped us off the map leaving no sign as to where we had gone. But the Lord took away all fear and gave us the joy of making friends, winning hundreds and thousands to the Lord and establishing dozens of churches all over that Communist-controlled province. Joshua 1:9 says, *"Have not I commanded thee? Be strong and of a good courage; be not afraid, neither be thou dismayed: for the Lord thy God is with thee whithersoever thou goest."*

The secret of it all was the love of God shed abroad in our hearts. The people soon learned that my wife and I loved them with a different kind of love that they had never known. They would welcome us into their humble little homes, have us drink tea with them, discuss their hearts' needs and we would just love them. They quickly forgot that we were Americans. We soon learned their down-to-earth needs. The Lord gave us delight in their language, customs and ways. It became so easy and natural to lead them to a true knowledge of the God of the heavens Who had come to earth. Jesus so loved them that He died for them and in triumph rose from the dead and lives to meet them in their far-off country villages and give them His very best, His own life. Earth can offer no pleasure, no joy like bowing with whole families as they turn from the futile things of earth, their pagan darkness, and accept Jesus as their personal Saviour.

The Lord was so good to give us three years together in that new home, but Jesus had something far better for my dear wife. He had a better home all prepared, so, after all those happy years together, He was calling her to that new home. Yes, "He goes to prepare a place for us," but there was no real way I could be prepared for the sorrow of her absence.

We had been visiting with Urb and his family in Siskiyou County, in Northern California for almost a month. Then we went to Williams, where Ivan lived. After a good visit there over Christmas of 1978, we came back home to Castro Valley. On February 2, 1979, Mary wasn't feeling well, so she went to the doctor for a checkup. Her blood count was low and because she was anemic, she went to the hospital for a blood transfusion. I stayed with her day and night. She got three pints of blood and the x-rays showed a malignant tumor in her stomach.

She didn't want to stay at the hospital, so I took her home and knew without a miracle she would be leaving for Glory Land soon. We prayed, anointed her with oil and did all we could but she became weaker in body, but, oh, so strong in the Lord, praising Him continually.

We had no assurance that we would have her here much longer. After nearly 59 years together in such joyous service, He was calling her home. We had big plans for the coming summer, but Jesus had bigger ones. And as the Apostle Paul said, "To depart and be with the Lord is far better."

The time was now approaching for me to go through the most devastating experience of all my life. My companion so steadfast and true was being called home. In the midst of the sorrow there was such joy. Then the time for our "goodbye" had arrived. Just before that chariot arrived to take her home she, though very weak, raised her hands to Heaven and with the last strength left in that precious body she said, "Praise the Lord, Hallelujah!" She exhaled one last time and then became still. She was gone. I went to the next room to wake my youngest son, Urb. He had driven 350 miles to be there for her departure. Urb came in and looked at his mother while I sat by the side of the bed. I put my head in my hands and cried triumphant sorrow. She had no pain, no distress; she was so at peace and on February 7, 1979, at around 2:00 a.m. the Lord said, "Well done, thou good and faithful servant. Enter thou into the joy of the Lord." She went to be with Him, at Whose side there are pleasures forever more. She was always saying "I will never cease to praise Him" and that is what she is doing now.

> *I saw her come to the river,*
> *With Canaan's land in view.*
>
> *Then Jesus took her by the hand,*
> *And led her right on through.*

On February 11, 1979, at the Cathedral at the Crossroads, friends and family of Mary Hall Travis gathered for a "Coronation Service" for this dear Saint of God who had already received her "Coronation Crown" in the presence of God.

The entire family participated in the service, praising God for the influence of her Christ-lived life. While her personal labor on earth had ended, the influence of her life upon her family and all she came in contact with continues.

Our son, Rev. Paul Travis, served as the officiating minister as he led the congregation in the singing of "O That Will Be Glory," and our daughter, Evangel, was at the piano. Ivan, our second son, sang some of the choruses the family had sung together when the children were young. Our eldest son Jonathan read one of Mary's favorite passages of scripture. He said that it was fitting that this should be a "Coronation Service" of praise and thanksgiving for the beautiful life lived before them. He was moved as he spoke of his mother. He spoke of the Vietnamese peoples' compassion and how living among them had an effect on him that caused him to be tender-hearted.

Then our youngest, Rev. Urban Travis, showed several slides of my precious Mary in Viet Nam doing what she loved best, meeting people and telling them of God's love for them. Paul's wife, Ruthie Travis, spoke on behalf of all the daughters-in-law. She read portions of Proverbs 31 commenting on verse 28. "Her children arise up, and call her blessed; her husband also, and he praiseth her." She also spoke of the great heritage bequeathed to the grandchildren.

There was a moment that particularly struck peoples' hearts. An elderly Vietnamese man tottered up to the podium near the end of the ceremony. I remembered him from our years in Viet Nam. He was among the million or so who had escaped in the massive evacuations of 1975. And here he was again to say a word, and his farewells at Mary's funeral.

He began, "of all the people I wish to give thanks for and give thanks to before I die, Mary Travis is one of them. I thank God for her and will continue to thank God for her until I see Him face to face...and see Mrs. Travis again." He then paused to gather himself before continuing. "I had my mother in Viet Nam. She is long gone. I was born to her, and I am grateful to her." He pointed at Mary in the coffin and said, "but that woman is my *spiritual* mother. Because of her I was born again. She left her homeland to come and tell me about my Saviour. Thanks to her I am a Christian."

As he stepped down from the podium, people were in awe over this man's final comments about Mary's well spent life. He was offered help as he descended the steps and walked across the front toward her coffin. With a single gesture he bowed to her, said goodbye and whispered, "thank you mother," and sat down.

I concluded the service remarking that what we saw in the casket was not Mary at all but the robe she wore. When I first saw it, it was beautiful, and though it was always beautiful to me, after years of use, it had become weathered and worn. She is not here, but with the One she loved, the Lord Jesus Christ who would give her a new body. Then I shared a poem that God had given me for this difficult time:

Mary My Dear

Comfort my heart with the fact dear Lord
That she really did arrive,
And now she's rejoicing with You, Dear Lord,
Not dead but truly alive.

All the trials of earth are past and gone
Now to rejoice ever more,
With Jesus, friends and loved ones again
Wonders of grace to explore.

I would not ask her back again
In this awful world of woe,
I want to go home there where she is
Where the wonders of God overflow.

She's laid aside this robe for a while
Erelong it will all be made new,
For Jesus is there to meet her
And He'll do what He said He'd do.

And one of these days, perhaps quite soon
When He comes again we'll meet,
O What a glorious day that will be
The joy of the Lord complete.

And throughout all the ages to come
We'll know as we are known,
At His side, pleasures beyond compare
To us will ever be shone.

—*C.E. Travis*

The Word says "...It is required in stewards, that a man be found FAITHFUL." This can be said of Mary Hall Travis. "Well done, thou good and FAITHFUL servant: enter thou into the joy of the Lord."[2]

Grady Mangham who had once been our Field Chairman in Viet Nam wrote the following in an "Obituary for Mary Travis" for the C&MA: "They worked and prayed and traveled and sang—together. Even poetry was often written jointly to express the deep longings and concerns of their souls for the land and people of their adoption—Viet Nam. Now Mary has gone ahead for a short while, but doubtless Chester is looking forward to a wonderful reunion in the presence of the Lord whom they both served so faithfully."

It is awfully lonesome without her, after so many years together, but how wonderful to know that we will soon be together again. Where there is no more parting, tears, or sorrows, exploring the wonders of God's grace forever. Even though I am awfully lonesome, I would never ask her back into this world of woe, and the dear Lord has faithfully sent the Comforter, who is holding and sustaining me in these trying days. So I will continue to praise Him Who doeth all things well.

As I sit in quiet meditation, it all seems like a dream. Praise the Lord, it's not a dream and it's not empty. Only the Lord's goodness could allow for us to join Him and make such a triumphant entry into that inheritance, incorruptible, undefiled, that fadeth not away, reserved in heaven.

She didn't have time to write a book
With paper and pen and ink,

While helpless souls were passing
Out over that awful brink.

No time for pictures and records
The emergency was on,
It was reach them now or never
They'd soon forever be gone.

Earthly pleasures were all so vain
Eternity was at hand,
The place where she could reach them
She was determined to stand.

So full of the love of Jesus
No plan to ever retire,
She went with that glorious message
Anointed with love and fire.

You'd find her in distant villages
Reaching the broken and lost,
Not thinking of ease or pleasure
And never counting the cost.

So on and on through night and day
To regions beyond she'd go,
To tell of Jesus' wondrous grace
And His loving kindness show.

The only treasures she wanted
Were those she had gained by love,

> *All her trophies were those redeemed*
> *Who welcomed her home above.*

> *Then there was that glorious day*
> *When Jesus said: "Come over here,*
> *And enter My joy forever*
> *With friends you have made so dear.*

There she is with that great cloud of witnesses, with a clear view, watching the conflict—especially those still back in Viet Nam, under the fiery trial that is on them. And I'm still here after 85 years of that good life in Jesus, while writing to you, expecting to take the next chariot home. Thanks be unto God for His unspeakable gift! This poem came over me while in silence with my Savior.

> *When every bridge is burned*
> *And every corner turned*
> *And we look back no more*
> *Then faith can operate*
> *And God becomes so great*
> *Our lord we then adore*

> *When shades of night come down*
> *And nature seems to frown*
> *We think we stand alone*
> *Just then we feel the touch*
> *Of One who loves so much*
> *The Lord is on the throne*

When we have lost our way
'Tis then we hear Him say
"I am the way, the life"
He guides from where we fail
Out from our dead end trail
And from our grief and strife

When fear and dread takes hold
And every voice is cold
It seems there's none to care
Then light comes shining through
From One so kind and true
Our Lord is always there

When sinking in despair
Where there's no word or prayer
Way out so far from land
One comes across the waves
He comes, He loves, He saves
He takes us by the hand

He knows the way we take
Each failure and mistake
He never leaves His own
So let us trust Him still
And live to do His will
Depend on Him alone

Then joy will come at last

While He still holds us fast
Our life will be complete
He'll take us over there
We'll in His glory share
Where friends and loved ones meet

28

Refiner's Fire

It had taken us many months together to type up Grandpa's memoirs. The sense of accomplishment was great when I finally typed the last page. I felt like we had completed a great thing but Grandpa's mind never quit thinking of more and more even after I had typed the final page. He continued making notes and reflected on the most recent years of his life on his own typewriter. Here are some of those pages.

I will lift up mine eyes unto the hills, from whence cometh my help. My help cometh from the LORD, which made heaven and earth. (Psalm 121:1-2) It's now 1984 and it goes without saying that the last five years of my life have been the hardest of all. Exiled from my chosen land and the absence of my dear wife of nearly 59 years together. Such happy memories. She is now rejoicing in the presence of the One who made life so meaningful during all our years together, but I am still here.

I have sold our little cottage house we lived in, which to me was not a home anymore since my "home-maker" was not there. I am now waiting for that next chariot with space available that I may take off to glory land where my loved ones dwell and to see Jesus, the One altogether lovely to my soul. The place is prepared and He has prepared the Way. "The Way of the Cross leads home." The saddest thing in all the world is that so many do not know the Way; JESUS.

I go out to the motor home and rejoice to be alone. After a lifetime walking through mobs of people, I don't have any problem being alone. Yet I could never have imagined the excruciating pain; the terrible void without my wife. I cry for the days when Mary and I were together, conversing and having a good time. I know it is temporary but the Lord is jealous over His children. This is another stage of weaning for me. This baby needs weaning even though he is old, and that weaning process is so painful. I cry to the Lord to draw me up close, and He does and I get a new vision of what it's all about. Weaning is from everything, even from every person, that He might have me for Himself alone.

Everything that was physically wrong with me in the past is now showing up in my "winter years." I've even lost a lot of marbles! I have a damaged heart valve, poor circulation and I lack strength. The old "chariot" has been swinging low quite often in the last few years but still has no space available so I'm still hanging around. This old "pumper" in my chest has been pumping away for 86 years and I thought it was ready to quit, but it still carries on and I don't get to go yet. In spite of the rugged way,

I have never had any time in my life when I have praised the Lord more for His loving kindness and tender mercy.

I used to go regularly to visit incoming Vietnamese refugees as they came into San Francisco, and at the Travis Airbase as they arrived from Hong Kong, Malaysia, and Viet Nam. I have had to slow down because I'm having my own "energy crisis," a power shortage. I am learning "in whatsoever state I am, therewith to be content." (Philippians 4:11) The Lord is so faithful and kind in His special care. I'm praising the Lord and I'll do it until my last breath!

Praising the Lord

Every breath that Jesus gives me
I will give it back, with praise,
That will be my occupation
Throughout all my living days.

Since He has done so much for me
What else can I ever do,
Such a faithful loving Saviour
To Him my Lord, I'll be true.

Apart from Him I'd have nothing
With Him, I have everything,
Oh the riches in Christ Jesus
With each breath His praise I'll sing.

He will be my theme forever
Through time and eternity,
I will never cease to praise Him
He has been so good to me.

As I travel in this world
I want folks to find out why,
I am always praising Jesus
So they'll join before they die.

May the number increase daily
As we join in joyful praise,
To the only one so worthy
Through all time and endless days.

Then throughout the endless ages
When this breath I'll need no more,
I will have new ways to praise Him
Jesus the Lord I adore.

This I will do until one of these days soon I will go where it is "far better" and there with a language with which I can praise, honor and glorify my precious Lord and Saviour I will do so as never before.

Grandpa had written his last memories but was quick to say, "Memories are great but the future is so much greater."

Crumbs from God's Table

When we're sitting at God's table
Feasting on the living bread,
Don't forget the millions hungry
Let crumbs fall that they be fed.

Bread of Life they've never tasted
While we've had more than we need,
Not a crumb has ever reached them
While they beg, and cry and plead.

Crumbs from God's great banquet table
Will abundantly supply,
All the food so sorely needed
So they will not starve and die.

God's harvest field, so bountiful
There are reapers everywhere,
But the gleaners are so hungry
Looking for some grain we share.

Handfuls we should drop on purpose
So that all may know God's love,
Through Christ Jesus our dear Saviour
God's great gift from heaven above.

Long ago God told His people
When they gather from the vine,
"Leave what's needed for the hungry
Let them eat, and taste new wine."

In this vineyard we can harvest
All the fruit that we may need,
God said, "Leave lots for the hungry"
Let our love be real indeed.

29

His Chariot Arrives

By the end of summer 1983, Grandpa's memoirs were typed out in a rough draft. I had gotten my needed grants and aids and was back in college and my life as a young student. I would still see Grandpa on weekends when I attended church, but my life went on and I never really thought much more about his memoirs that we had worked on together for so many hours. But the stories I had typed up while spending time with Grandpa had an impact on my life that would prove to be lasting.

Urb's oldest son, Drew, took off a couple of years between his college and seminary studies and moved in to help care for his grandfather in his advanced years. Urb's second son, Drake, would visit from Simpson on the weekends. Grandpa was deteriorating fast. In his final season of life, he noted to his grandsons, "I have learned more about the Lord in these last two years of my life while lying flat on my back than the prior 70 years serving Him." He always wanted more time with Jesus.

His grandsons recall that their Grandpa who was once so strong and clear-headed and coy and humorous struggled for breath and longed for the pain to subside. He used to eat with the family and eat like a trooper he did. Now a cracker and four ounces of broth gave him a wretched stomachache. His body was worn out. We ached to see this legend fade away knowing that he would soon leave us for another world.

Chester Travis passed away peacefully on September 23, 1984, while living in the home of his son, Paul and daughter-in-law, Ruthie, in Hayward, California. I had gone on to finish school. I remember Ruthie calling to tell me that Grandpa had passed away. She knew we were close and wanted to tell me personally and I remember how grateful I was for that.

Drew was at his side and still remembers it clearly, "He was gone. His body was there but he was gone. At times like this we remember one of Grandpa's favorite verses was 'to be absent from the body is to be present with the Lord.' This was his vital, firm and living hope the last few months of his life.

At the time I was a young college graduate not sure of what the next step was going to be in my life. My bedroom was down the hall from Grandpa at Uncle Paul's home. I was doing part time youth ministry and carpentry work. I was a young man trying to find the Lord's direction for his life. During those years I spent many hours in Grandpa's room. We would talk of a variety of subjects from football to theology to missions. He didn't understand what American culture had become with all its problems, wealth, entertainment and fascination with externals. His simple rural faith in Christ had led him to Moody Bible Institute and on to French Indo-China in 1925. God's Word and Christ Himself had sustained him and Mary through wars, prison camp and all the rigors of missions in that remote land. He was not impressed with glamour, glitz or show. He loved John's words in 1 John 2:17, 'the man who does the will of God lives forever.' Earthly things meant nothing to him. 'Trust and Obey' was his favorite hymn. He believed this old song carried the heart and soul of the Christian life.

"He always loved his wife Mary passionately though his irrepressible humor often clashed with her stately deportment. He revered God's Word and would never place anything on top of his Bible. All these memories and more flooded through my mind when I found Grandpa. He was gone. His body was there but he was gone. 'to be absent from the body is to be present with the Lord.'"

Dr. Louis King, who had become the President of The Christian and Missionary Alliance, wrote the following note to Paul after hearing of Chester's passing. "Today the word has come that your dear father has departed to be with Jesus. This is just a note, but I did want you to know how very much I appreciated your father. His utter dedication, more than fifty years of valiant service, and success in winning the lost to Christ has been an inspiration to me and a host of others. The Christian and Missionary Alliance and the Evangelical Church of Viet Nam were honored to have him as one of our number. I have happy memories of his poetry and the rich and delightful vein of humor that so characterized him."

Dr. Mark Lee, long-time president of Simpson College attended the funeral services, representing the Division of Overseas Ministries for the C&MA added, "New York feels that it has lost one of the greatest missionaries ever to have served in our society."

Later I read this article published in The Alliance Witness magazine, now the Alliance Life, titled "He Would Not Quit." His friend, Rev. Eugene Evans wrote: "One could use several adjectives to describe this old warrior — committed, determined, fearless, stubborn, loving, witty. But the one that perhaps most aptly describes Chester Travis is unique. Indeed there were few like him.

"Saved at age 14, later called to missions and influenced by Rev. Paul Rader, then president of the C&MA, to service with the Alliance, Chester Travis and his wife, Mary, sailed for French Indo-China in 1925.

"Mr. Travis was known throughout every province he served. He and his wife, also now deceased, would pack up their homemade house trailer, set a homemade alarm to protect his home and head for the country. He was a true jack-of-all-trades; the American military which would come to know and love him, called him a 'bailing-wire genius.' He was an itinerant preacher and church planter. His 'flock' was widely scattered, but he eventually visited all of them on one of his extended itineraries.

"It was Chester and Mary Travis who reached the ancient Cham people for the first time. During World War II they were interned by the Japanese in the southern delta and were later repatriated on the famous Swedish ship, *Gripsholm*, in 1943. But they went back to Viet Nam. Nothing, not even war, could keep them from returning to their adopted land.

"The average term of service for missionaries is four years. But then Chester Travis was not an average missionary. When he reached the end of his 'last' four-year term, he just stayed on the field. Go home? Where was home? Viet Nam, that is where home was! He was already past retirement age and going on his sixth year without furlough. For his own physical well-being the field committee begged him to take a furlough. The wily, old saint knew if he returned to the States well beyond the age of 65 he would never get back to his beloved Vietnamese people. So he stayed. And stayed. Finally, after 12 years of continuous service without a furlough, he was persuaded to return to the States.

"The Mission arranged for Chester and his wife to return home by boat—the same way they first went to Viet Nam in 1925. Missionaries in Saigon went down to the dock to see them off. They all engaged in the usual small talk that precedes such last goodbyes. This was it! He was leaving, never to return. His eyes filled with tears. With a quick and final handshake, he turned, walked the plank and entered his cabin. And the curtain came down on 50 years of service in Viet Nam.

"At 86 years of age his 'old ticker' finally gave out. He would not quit, but his heart did. He entered the presence of the Lord whom he faithfully served for 72 years.

"Another great pioneer missionary is gone, but the fruits of his labors remain. There will be many who will rise up and call him blessed."

In fashion so like Chester Travis, he wrote the following poem that was befitting the order of service at his own funeral. When I first read it, I somehow knew that not even death could keep him from telling others about his Lord and Saviour, Jesus Christ.

With Him

This tattered robe I do not need,
Just lay it aside with care.
I will be away at that time,
With my dear Lord over there.

So don't you cry as if no hope
For I'm coming back again,
With Jesus Christ the mighty King
And see Him reign, among men.

This vesture He will make all new
In great glory like His own,
Death swallowed up in victory
As He reigns upon His throne.

So be you ready for that day
Caught with Him in the air,
Together with Him forever
His love and glory we'll share.

Therefore, be steadfast in the Lord
Abounding in love and grace,
And when He comes to earth again
You'll have a glorious place.

And we'll reign with Him forever
As He wipes all tears away,
With Him there's no more sorrow
In that glorious endless day.

30

A Final Connection

Years after Chester and Mary Travis left the Viet Nam field the impact of their ministry was still evident. The door had closed on that era when missionaries were allowed in the country of Viet Nam, and it was difficult for those missionaries to understand the Lord's working at the time. For us looking back, decades later, His plan is easy to see. The national church of Viet Nam was strong. They had leaders, they had a president and they didn't need the missionaries there. God moved them out of the way so the pastors and churches of Viet Nam could do their work. In April of 1975, when the missions had to pull out, there were reportedly 50,000 Christians in Viet Nam. Today there are millions of believers, with minimal missionary presence. According to *Operation World*, there are over 8 million people adhering to Christendom as of 2010. Indeed, the field is strong today because of the work the pioneer missionaries like the Travis' and many others accomplished.

I knew first-hand the impact the story of the Travis'

had made on my life but it would be years before I would hear some of the following stories about how they touch others' lives during their years in Viet Nam. On one occasion Evan Evans and Tom Mangham, son of Grady Mangham, wanted to prepare an audio-visual for a missionary meeting. They gathered some marvelous missionary slides and background music. Then they decided they needed a song with a call for recruits. So Evans and Mangham wrote this song:

Who Will Answer?

From shore to shore,
From sea to sea,
The world revolves in apathy.
A man and wife, all bent and gray,
Stay on and on to show the way,
And when at last they have to leave,
They just return to grieve and grieve.
Who will answer?
When the soul is darkened?
With a fear that cannot save?
Who will go and tell them
This is why the Saviour came?
Who will answer?

The song they wrote was based on the true story of Chester and Mary Travis who had spent a lifetime in Viet Nam, and when it came time for them to retire, they did not want to go because there was no one to take their place.[1]

Another story about how they had touched the lives of so many is told by Anne Stebbins Moore. Anne, grew up with several of the Travis children and she remembered her own personal experience: "I was Art Director of The Alliance Life, then called The Alliance Witness. My work involved making weekly trips to Spectratone Color Lab, a well-known supplier of quality prints and film from slides.

"The first time I walked into Spectratone and nervously handed my business card to the man on duty, his face lit up. 'The Christian and Missionary Alliance! Do you know a missionary by the name of Chester Travis?' To which I replied, 'Yes, I knew him well.' Spectratone Color Lab was founded and owned by three Viet Nam war vets. That day they began sharing with me an amazing story.

"Their first assignment to Viet Nam, their battleship docked at Nha Trang and the soldiers were ordered to wade ashore. Totally exposed, they were terrified, having visions of being fired at and killed before they could reach dry land. But they made it. They began walking down a Nha Trang street when suddenly an old jalopy car pulled up next to them. A friendly American voice called out, 'Where are you guys headed? Would you like a ride?' It was as though an angel had suddenly appeared from the skies.

"I can't remember if the infantrymen were free to accept Chester Travis' kind invitation or if they felt compelled to stay with their company. But I do know this was the beginning of a great and lasting friendship. The three, at least two of them Jews, spent many happy times in the Travis home. Their gratitude to Chester Travis and his wife was boundless.

"Needless to say, I was treated with great respect, and given excellent professional service by these owners of *Spectratone* who had been the recipients of such kindness and grace."

Tom Stebbins, also shared remembering about their service to the Lord, "I knew Chester and Mary Travis intimately for about thirty years. 'Mavericks' is the first word that comes to mind when I think of this godly, impassioned, creative, unique couple. Though intensely loyal to their denomination and the Viet Nam Mission, they were also independent thinkers who were unconcerned about what people thought of them. They were totally abandoned to do what God through His Word directed them to do. No price was too high to pay, no sacrifice too great to make in order to bring the Good News of Jesus Christ's saving grace to the Vietnamese people whom they loved unconditionally and ardently!"

I had no idea my life would ever intersect with Grandpa's again. He had been gone many years and now more than twenty years later I'm no longer a young student but married with my own family and living in Marietta, Georgia. I live many miles and years from those college days in California. My years at college are a very distant past, and as with most people, only keeping in touch with a select few from those years gone by.

Along with my family I attend a local C&MA church here in Marietta where I've taught Sunday school and have been actively involved for many years. One of my family's favorite times each year is during Missionary Convention week at our church. We hear updates and stories from missionaries from around the world. The church spends weeks planning, praying, preparing, and decorating for the events to come. There are mini-conventions for the kids and time each night to mingle and talk with each missionary there. We also have a bookstore during Convention week and get a chance to buy and read stories about other wonderful missionary lives.

It was always during this time each year I'd begin to wonder what ever happened to Chester and Mary Travis' story. I saw many other missionary stories published, would I someday see theirs published? I could still remember many of the stories and felt sure that someone in the family would have it published. One publishing company began to publish a series of C&MA missionary stories entitled "The Jaffray Collection of Missionary Portraits." I was sure I'd see their powerful story published and on the bookshelf anytime.

The Lord laid their story on my heart each year, during our Missionary Convention, as I wondered what happened to it, where it was, and whether or not it would be published. I looked forward to this week each year but soon I started to dread it because I knew the Lord would prick my heart. But each year I'd push the thoughts out of my mind telling myself it wasn't *my* responsibility.

Finally during one convention when we had someone from the Alliance National Office at our convention, I asked how I might find out what happened to their story. I took my first step when I contacted the C&MA archive department, in Colorado Springs, to see if their memoirs were on file. I felt that at least then I'd know it was preserved and someone had their story on file to do something with. Maybe not being published was okay if it was at least somewhere safe. To my great disappointment, the archive department didn't have anything written about the Travis story. They gave me current address information for family members so I could contact them. Paul, Urb and even Drake who I remembered so well but what exactly was I supposed to say? Again I pushed the thoughts from my mind because it wasn't really *my* responsibility. The Travis family was large enough and surely someone was capable of doing something with their story. It wasn't my family and it really wasn't any of my business. Was it?

During those years in my life, my family would be dealt our own hand of grief when my husband's younger sister died unexpectedly. Our own faith was tried and tested and as a result deepened. We began to see life from a whole new perspective, and view the few precious years we were given as a window of opportunity to accomplish the Lord's will for lives.

As I mentioned earlier, in my experience when I make plans without submitting them to the Lord, they rarely work out. The best laid plans are the Lord's and *my* plans are not always His plans. Now with a few more years of life experiences behind me, I had also learned about submitting my life to the will of the Lord.

The next year as our Missionary Convention time drew closer, I began to feel the pangs of the Chester Travis story. I was in the middle of Beth Moore's Bible study, *Believing God*, and I knew it was time for me to take that step of faith and trust in the Lord's leading. In complete surrender to the Lord it was time for me to act. Weeks before our Missionary Convention even began I finally wrote to Chester's son, Urb, telling him of my convictions, and how I felt the Lord wanted to use me, if only to prompt the family to action. I didn't know where it would all lead but I knew now I would take each step in obedience. I wasn't even certain that the family would remember me from so many years ago. I finally mailed the letter and was filled with a peace I hadn't felt in years about the whole thing. That was the last I expected to hear about it.

Our Missionary Convention week had started at church and I was enjoying one of the sweetest weeks of spiritual filling. Then right in the middle of our Missionary Convention week I received a phone call from Rev. Paul Travis, the pastor whose home I'd lived in so many years before. What timing!

Paul couldn't clearly remember who I was, (he was now in his 70's) or how I would even knew of his father's memoirs. Up until that point I had never shared with anybody about the story I had typed up so many years before. Paul confessed that his father's story and papers were in a box in his storage unit and he had never even read them. Paul had no idea what his father had written. As we talked on the phone, story after story flooded my memory and I began to share them with Paul. I had remembered how Paul's child-like faith had taught his parents a lesson in the trust and care of the Lord. I remembered the funny stories and the sacrifices they had made giving up everything to serve where the Lord called them to serve. Mostly I remembered how his life had touched mine in such a special way and showed me what living a life in complete surrender to the Lord looked like.

Incredibly I had typed his father's memoirs 23 years earlier while living in Hayward, California (across the country from where I now live), and now they were sitting in storage in Jacksonville, Florida just a few hours' drive from me. The Lord had worked out His perfect timing in putting all the pieces together so I could easily get my hands on the beginning of this book; the manuscript I had typed up with Grandpa. I knew instantly that it was all orchestrated by God and brought together for a purpose. Now I had the faith to trust the Lord with each step to come.

That led me to the second part of my journey to help tell this touching story of Chester and Mary Travis. I had never written a book before and I knew nothing about publishing. The thing I *did* know for certain was that this was clearly something the Lord put on my heart and was leading me to do. I knew the voice of God when He called me to this project, and I knew if He called me, He would equip me and He would complete it! This was His plan which was far beyond what I could have imagined and I was only to be His faithful servant in obedience.

The story of Chester and Mary Travis is so moving it was forever stamped on my heart in the early 1980's, and I believe all those who read it will also be touched in some way. It's a story with a message for missions, for surrender and serving the Lord, wherever you're called to serve. I'm absolutely convinced this is a story that the Lord wanted told and I'm humbled to be His servant.

Now unto the King eternal,
immortal, invisible,
the only wise God,
be honor and glory
forever and ever.
Amen.

1 Timothy 1:17

Photo Gallery

*Young Mary who captured
the heart of Chester in 1919*

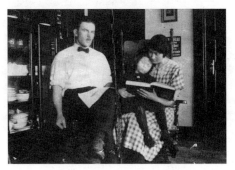

*Home in Nyack in 1924,
waiting for word to leave*

*Early Mission Conference in 1928,
Chester holding Jonathan, Mary next
to him (second row, far left)*

*Chester, Mary, Ivan, Jonathan,
Evangel and Paul in 1933*

*Travis family during
their first furlough of 1931*

Chester with his four boys in about 1934

*Family picture taken in 1934 shortly after
the birth of Urban, the youngest*

*Mary with baby Urban
born in 1934*

Family photo around 1937
(Front row: Paul, Ike, Urb and Jonathan)

First trailer Chester built in 1934, used to travel
and camp among the Vietnamese people

*The Model A used up for the Lord
during the first term on the field*

Family photo in about 1938

*Spring of 1938, family dressed
in Vietnamese attire*

*Family photo in about 1938
(Front row: Urb, Paul, Ike and Jonathan)*

Taken in 1944 – Back row: John Hall,
Jonathan Hall (Mary's father), Urban,
Nettie Hall (Mary's mother), Lon Hall
Front row: Evie Hall, Mary Hall Travis, Gela Hall

The Gripsholm *where the Travis*
family were repatriated in
1944 from World War II interment

Family photo some time after their repatriation
(Back row: Ike, Jonathan, Paul, Urb)

	Ivan	Evangel	Urban	
Jonathan		Mary	Chester		Paul

Pictured around 1949 before heading
back to Viet Nam with just the youngest, Urban

*Young Urban working with his parents in the
Delta after graduating from Dalat School*

*Chester and Mary make recordings for
their phonograph and radio projects*

*Urb and Chester with a newer
vehicle and a PA system on top!*

*The Mercury and second trailer used by
the Travis family in the 1950's & 1960's*

Chester perched on the back of the trailer.

Picture of a typical open air meeting
with Chester and Mary
"Tin-Lanh" meaning Gospel
written on the sides

*Chester follows the Lord's lead
and ministers from a boat.*

*Chester helping a man to "breath easy"
as he was now safe in the Lord's hands
after Baptism*

Chester with two Vietnamese girls.

Returning for a final term,
From 1962—1975

Chester at an open market

Typical scene at a Baptismal Service in Viet Nam

*Another Baptismal scene with many young
Vietnamese children*

TO OUR OWN DEAR ONES
Christmas 1965

We all rejoice on Christmas Day
    That Christ our Lord was born;
He left His heav'nly home on high,
    What matchless love was shown.

Though royal born, no crown He wore,
    No place of fame He sought,
But love impelled Him to the cross,
    Our ransom there He bought.

So let us not forget the price
    These happy Christmas days
But honor Him for His great gift
    With songs of endless praise.

And 'specially at this Christmas time
    We think of YOU so dear
Though far away, our hearts rejoice
    In Him we're always near.
            Love, Mom + Dad

*Mary and Chester's Christmas photo
and poem from 1965.*

Mary at her desk, taken in 1968.

1968 laying the corner stone for
a new church at Nhon Thanh Village!

Another happy gathering by the river side.

*Honored guests at a ceremony
for a departing Chaplain.*

Chester and Mary visiting with the U.S. Military,
Chaplains helping build a church!

Mary on her way out to the market.

Chester does a wee bit of coal shopping.

*Soldiers pausing at the graves
of martyred missionaries
during TET '68*

*Taken in front of a home
in Viet Nam.*

Written on the back – "Dad with his wreck."

Beyond Retirement

*Chester and Mary are not ready to
leave their beloved Viet Nam.*

*Picture taken during some of their
final years in Viet Nam.*

*Chester and Mary with a
Vietnamese friend.*

*Home in the U.S. enjoying
the travels of the Motor Home.*

Chester always full of character!

⚬ *Bibliography of Sources* ⚬

Chapter 3: The Call and a Companion

1. *Moody Bible Institute Information,*
   http://re.moody.edu/GenMoody/default.asp?Section
   ID=FD16FFDD8F144A9E8FF9696F36331E58

Chapter 4: Preparation for the Ministry

1. Drake Travis, *Christ our Healer Today:
   The Ministry of Healing in the Christian
   and Missionary Alliance.*
   (Camp Hill, PA: Christian Publications, Inc, 1996)

2. *Alliance Theological Seminary information:*
   http://www.alliance.edu/?page=ATSHistory

3. E.F. Irwin, *With Christ in Indo-China*
   (Harrisburg, PA: Christian Publications, Inc., ca. 1937)

4. Irving R. Stebbins, *Pioneering with Christ in Vietnam*
   (Fort Lauderdale, FL: Winning Publishers, 2006)

5. A.W. Tozer, *Let My People Go: The Life of
   Robert A. Jaffray (Jaffray Collection of Missionary
   Portraits)*
   (Camp Hill, PA: Christian Publications, Inc., 1990)

Chapter 5: To Viet Nam

1. Stuart Murray, *Eyewitness Vietnam War*,
   (New York, NY: DK Publishing, Inc., 2005)

2. *Nha Trang, Vietnam Information*,
   http://www.vietscape.com/travel/nhatrang/index.
   html

Chapter 6: Spreading the News

1. E.F. Irwin, *With Christ in Indo-China*, (Harrisburg,
   PA: Christian Publications, Inc., ca. 1937)

2. *Dalat, Vietnam Information*,
   http://www.terragalleria.com/vietnam/vietnam.
   da-lat.html

Chapter 12: Back Again

1. Charles Long, *To Vietnam with Love: The Story
   of Charlie & E.G. Long (Jaffray Collection of
   Missionary Portraits)*
   (Camp Hill, PA: Christian Publications, Inc., 1995)

2. Ibid.

Chapter 17: Three Years of Internment

1. *Teia Maru Ship*,
   http://rasputin.physics.uiuc.edu/~wiringa/Ships/
   MS-3/Japan/TeiaMaru.html

2. *Exchange Liner*,
   http://www.salship.se/mercy.asp

3. Ibid.

Chapter 19: Work in the Delta

1. Stuart Murray, *Eyewitness Vietnam War*,
   (New York, NY: DK Publishing, Inc., 2005)

2. Ibid.

3. *The Call of Vietnam*,
   Official publication of the Vietnam Mission
   of The Christian and Missionary Alliance.

Chapter 20: Buying up Opportunities

1. Stuart Murray, *Eyewitness Vietnam War*,
   (New York, NY: DK Publishing, Inc., 2005)

2. Grady & Evelyn Mangham, *Oasis*
   (unpublished family book)

Chapter 21: Loud Speakers for the Lord

1. James C. Hafley, *To Live or To Die*
   (Grand Rapids, MI: Zondervan Publishing House, 1969)

2. Ibid.

3. Stuart Murray, *Eyewitness Vietnam War*,
   (New York, NY: DK Publishing, Inc., 2005)

Chapter 23: Beyond Retirement

1. James C. Hafley, *To Live or To Die*
   (Camp Hill, PA: Christian Publications, Inc.,)

Chapter 24: TET Offensive of 1968

1. Charles Long, *To Vietnam with Love: The Story of Charlie & E.G. Long (Jaffray Collection of Missionary Portraits)*
   (Camp Hill, PA: Christian Publications, Inc., 1995)

2. James C. Hafley, *To Live or To Die*
   (Grand Rapids, MI: Zondervan Publishing House, 1969)

3. Charles Long, *To Vietnam with Love: The Story of Charlie & E.G. Long (Jaffray Collection of Missionary Portraits)*
   (Camp Hill, PA: Christian Publications, Inc., 1995)

4. James C. Hafley, *To Live or To Die*
    (Grand Rapids, MI: Zondervan Publishing House, 1969)

5. James C. Hafley, *To Live or To Die*
    (Grand Rapids, MI: Zondervan Publishing House, 1969)

Chapter 26: Our Time's Up

1. Information from Grady & Evelyn Mangham, previous Field Director to Viet Nam.

Chapter 27: The Upward Call

1. Letter from C&MA archive files

2. Information of Mary's funeral service was taken from the C&MA archive files

Epilogue

1. Grady & Evelyn Mangham, *Oasis*
    (unpublished family book)

Acknowledgements

It has been a special blessing for me to be involved in putting together this book about the lives of Chester and Mary Travis.

Thank you, Paul and Ruthie Travis, who took me in many years ago in 1983 as a college student who needed a place to live. There you guided me spiritually as a Pastor and wife and gave me the opportunity and privilege of knowing Rev. Chester Travis, whom I called "Grandpa." Then Paul, you became my biggest supporter and believed in me as I worked to bring this story together for publication.

A huge thank you to Leslie Travis Hall. Without your encouragement I feel certain that your grandfather would never have taken time to write down his memoirs in the first place. And for your countless hours of tape recording trying to get the "details" from your grandfather so it wouldn't be lost. I think you truly "started the ball rolling," so to speak and I'm sure the family will be forever grateful for that.

Thank you to so many who guided me along the way giving me information as to who to talk to and where to find answers. Also, to some of my closest friends and accountability partners who've been a constant encouragement and support to keep me going from the very beginning of this project: Debbie Norman, Kelly Mulroy, Debbie Windham, and Sue Schultz. You gave me the encouragement to complete what I was called to do and saw the vision as I did.

I can't go without thanking several of the "saints" who served in Viet Nam themselves, or grew up there as children and aided me in filling in several gaps of information and details: Betty Stebbins Gibbs, Tom Stebbins, Anne Stebbins Moore and Grady and Evelyn Mangham. Also the sweet ladies at the C&MA Archive Department, your help was immeasurable.

I would be remiss not to say to Drake Travis, thank you for introducing me to your wonderful family in the first place. You gave me a glimpse of the treasure you have, and then were a faithful friend in your support in completing this.

Most importantly I have to thank my family. My children who have allowed me to give of my time to write and work on this project, thank you Kimberly, Kaitlin and Joey. I am proud to be your mom. Always cling to the Word, and the Lord will bring about great victories in your lives. Also to my supportive husband who seemed to know as instinctively as I did that I was called to this project and supported me to the end. Ed you make me the better person that I am and I love you.

Thank you to the entire Travis family for allowing me the privilege of getting to know and love Chester Travis. He had an incredible impact on my life all those years ago and I'm confident countless others along the way. This was a project I had helped him start in 1983 and now the Lord has been gracious in letting me do my part to bring it full circle. Chester, you were the "Grandpa" that filled my heart with the Lord.

Author:
Trena Chellino

Help Viet Nam Today

The Travis family continues to be a part of the work in Viet Nam through the Good Samaritan Medical Dental Ministry (GSMDM) which was founded by Dr. Vien Doan. Dr. Doan was born in Nha Trang – the same town as Urban Travis. Dr. Doan got his medical degree in the U.S. and has dedicated his life to going back to his home country to show the love of Christ to the people of Viet Nam.

Each year since the Summer of 2000 The Good Samaritans travel to remote villages in Viet Nam to provide needed healthcare for the poorest of the poor. Generally, in a two week period the team will exam and treat over 4,000 patients, providing services such as medical, surgical, dental and optometric services. They are complemented by a full service labs, EKG, ultrasound.

There are 2 teams. The Primary Care Team consists of physicians, dentists, pharmacists, nurses and student volunteers. The student volunteers are not required to have medical experiences but will be trained to assist the healthcare providers to ensure the clinics run smoothly and efficiently. The Primary Care team will treat all patients within their scope of practice and those patients required specialized care will be referred to the Surgical Team that will come the following week.

The Surgical Team consists of surgical specialists and operating room nurses. This team brings with them their own supplies and equipment. They work in conjunction with local surgeons out of Provincial Hospitals to care for these patients at the same time share their skills with the local physicians.

The team goes even further for those patients that can't be cared for while the team is there for the 2 weeks. Typically these patients are young children suffering from life-threatening illnesses such as Congenital Heart Defects. These children are sponsored by the team, all expenses paid, to have their surgeries done by specialized heart centers in Hanoi, Hue or Saigon.

In addition to the Summer Mission, GSMDM has developed an educational institute for the training of doctors including the speciality of Emergency Medicine. There are plans for building a state-of-the-art hospital facility in Viet Nam one day as well.

A portion of the proceeds from the book sales of *Love Poured Out for Viet Nam* will go to GSMDM and their on-going work in Viet Nam. Find out more about GSMDM at gsmedicalministry.org.

Dr. Vien Doan, founder of GSMDM, returns to Nha Trang and sees an old school photo that officials shared with him.

GSMDM Team 2005 included Urban, his wife, Liz, and son, Drake Travis.

Urban Travis presents a quilt as a gift to a mother and her young girl who will be receiving surgery to repair a cleft palate. Urban has traveled with GSMDM several times to help translate.

Serena and Drake, grandson of Chester and Mary Travis, entertain Vietnamese kids while parents are receiving treatment.

Josiah, great-grandson of Chester and Mary Travis, helped on a GSMDM trip in 2006.

Three generations of the Travis family: Urban Travis, Emily (Urb's grand-daughter), and Serena (Urb's daughter-in-law) serving with GSMDM in 2012.

Living Stones Publications

Living Stones Publications is a division of Divine Sign Productions. Drake and Serena are dedicated to producing God-honoring content in various media forms.

Love Poured Out for Viet Nam is also available in print and audiobook.

Books by Dr. Drake W. Travis
Healing Power, Voice Activated
Poder Para Sanar En Su Voz

See more books and content at **www.drakeandserena.com**.